On the Head of a Pin by J. Nelson Leith

Published by Cenolithic

johnnelsonleith@gmail.com

ON THE HEAD OF A PIN

a hardboiled detective fable

J. Nelson Leith

O paladins, the lesson for today

Is how to be unhappy yet polite.

Robert Frost

"The Lesson for Today"

ACT I

PART ONE

The most dangerous part of dancing with angels is that one of Them is Death.

That's not to say the rest of Them are innocent little cherubs. Far from it. A Sufi chick named Núr once told me, "*Ëayyan-Alláh likul shay' malakan*," which (roughly translated) means that God made an angel for everything there is. Rain, concrete, jealousy, cars, hard liquor, the dark of night, you name it. Any one of those can be dangerous. Even more so when they gang up on you.

But, especially because their respective angels all know Death, and She likes to be introduced to Her friends' acquaintances. She insists on it, eventually. She can be very assertive.

There's a wide spectrum of definitiveness for the messengers, I was told.

It breaks down until even the most specific and inconsequential thing has its dancing partner. There's an angel for revolvers, and one for every individual piece of heat, or so Núr would have you believe.

Does a drop of strawberry ice cream that stained a silk blouse in Central Park at 11:45 a.m. on Independence Day, 1928, have its own angel? You bet.

Granted, angels *that* definitive aren't very interesting. Little more than will-o'-wisps that flutter in and out of existence like exotic leptons in a particle accelerator.

The really interesting ones are those who govern whole categories of things, the ones you might worship as gods if you were ignorant or just wanted to piss off the Likeness, angels like Fire and Strength and Healing and Invention.

And the Seven Sisters—those Pleiádes of Sin—who, of course, throw the wildest bashes in the other world.

»-«

I was at one of the Sisters' shindigs, at Núr's insistence, when I learned about the PIN.

Contrary to the conventions of the genre, Núr Lucas did not strut into my detective agency sporting a fur-trimmed coat, too much lipstick, and a dubious story about a missing husband. I did not first see her ample curves in silhouette through the etched glass of my office door, where the scraped-away block letters of a dead partner's name were still barely visible.

I never had a partner. I'm not much of a team player, I guess. My business is named for me alone: C. R. Oliver Investigations. My "X" is the only one on the deed and the business license. If I ever had a partner who got waxed while pursuing a case, I would have chalked it up to the way things work in the Private Eye business instead of cultivating a vendetta and the traditional detective's booze habit.

You want to know how I take my drink? In moderation, because *I own* the bottle. The bottle does not own me.

No, contrary to convention, Núr emailed me through my website and invited me to discuss a potential case at her spa.

> From: nurlucas256
> Subject: "Client inquiry"
>
> Mr. Oliver,
> I hope this message finds you in good health and good fortune. My name is Núr Lucas and I have a situation developing which I believe might be ideally suited to your particular talents, based on the website's description of your business history.
>
> I would prefer to meet you at my place of business, assuming you are taking new cases. I can keep sundown to midnight open for you tonight or tomorrow. The address is 786 Palm.

That end of Palm Avenue was in an artsy, gentrified neighborhood called Sutler Heights, the sort of tight and cluttered junk drawer where a city once stashed away its Blacks or immigrants, later repurposed as a Mecca for trust-fund brats burning off White guilt by thrusting themselves into their grandparents' social purgatory—and, of course, the multi-cultural camp followers who make a living off them.

Originally the haunt of hash dealers, speak-easies, and rollicking jazz daddy-o's from the rough side of town, Sutler Heights was now, in 2007, an incubator for head shops selling everything but weed, fully legal bars, and casually sad singer-guitarists from the squeaky clean burbs.

It was a Safe New World.

And, that's just fine as far as I'm concerned. Despite my line of work, I'm no tough looking to get a sock in the jaw for my daily bread. I wearied quick of that habit growing up in a brutal, backwoods Dogpatch where shotguns were considered legit fireworks and half-wild, redneck brats thought cracking each other's skulls open with thrown rocks was a team sport, best played against kids who weren't lucky enough to have a team.

No, I much prefer the mode of a city that's already been pummeled into a calm, civil middle age, where the teams of which I was not a member took out their aggressions through the etiquette of politics, and the social sports consist primarily of conspicuous hipsterdom and assiduously constructed respectability.

The more conspicuous or well-constructed, the better.

Núr's Sutler Heights was the local hipster stadium. My own neighborhood started as an immigrant shanty town, unofficially labeled Bohunk Manor before the city scooped it up during an annexing craze. Today, it's a conservative suburb called Lobany Place, a well-sewn mask of propriety stretched tight over the seedy skull of its past.

The row where my detective's office sits was a string of dope dens back in the Jazz Age, but now it's anchored at either end by a Christian bookstore and a plastic surgeon: one-stop shopping for self-improvement inside and out.

I looked out the display window of my office. It needed cleaning outside, or a good hard rain. The restaurant across the street was filling up its outside tables, and I could see shadows on the street of the people eating on the rooftop patio.

I opened the second desk drawer. My pistol was sleeping there in an open, velvet-lined case, like a cursed prince in an inside-out fairy tale. Wouldn't need that. Not today, not in this city.

I slid the drawer closed and clacked out a brief response: "Be there to discuss this evening." Send.

»-«

Núr's place was a long, peaceful walk from my office: starting where Dogwood crosses Pine, up Pine Street and past the cemetery on Fig Lane, and finally into Sutler Heights on Palm Avenue. The spa snuggled between a consignment shop and a Salvadoran diner.

An electronic chime gonged when I opened the door. The waiting area was all beige and eggshell, and stank of saffron. On the desk was a plastic jar, half-full of money, the label reading: *Every Day We're Closer To The Cure*. Leaning against the wall was—of course, I thought—a rain stick.

A coolly inaccessible little hostess squatted froglike on a wicker stool behind the desk, wearing blue leggings and a loosely knit Andean sweater that looked like it was meant to be worn by two of her. Without looking up from her paperback of Anne Sexton poems, she waved me toward the meditation room.

I stepped to follow her wave, but remembered that I was a detective, stepped back, and leaned on the counter.

"You don't want to know who I am or why I'm here?"

As she peered over the top of the paperback at me, her fingers shifted on the cover, showing more letters. I had guessed wrong. It was a book on anti-sexism politics.

"You're Charles Roland Oliver," her hidden mouth spoke while bored, holly-green eyes looked unblinkingly into mine. "You're a private detective, and you're here because my boss is a crazy woman."

Apparently, she had been forewarned of my arrival.

"Crazy, huh? Aren't you afraid I might share that with her?"

My elbow bumped against the charity jar.

She sighed.

"She knows what I think. I just work here for the free yoga."

She set the book down, resigned to the conversation. Now I could see the entire title: *Anti-Sexual Polemics*. I had been doubly wrong.

She slipped one leg out of the cross they were in, letting it dangle carelessly. The wicker stool made a cozy, creaking sound as she moved, like an old sailing ship rolling in a swell.

"Is this where you try to get something out of me about her, rather than going in and asking her yourself?"

"Huh. You read more than politics."

She looked at nothing to her left.

"I don't read politics."

She looked at me again and put the tip of one finger on her book.

"This is about literary criticism."

"Well, I'm not doing the typical detective thing here, if that's what you mean. I simply didn't want to be rude and just—"

She picked up the book again, opened it, found her page, and covered her mouth with it as even-more-bored eyes glared at me over the top. Then, she hid her whole face.

I stepped back, off the counter.

"Is it for or against?"

"What?" she asked from behind the paperback.

"The book. Is it for or against anti-sexual polemics?"

"It's not politics, it's criticism. It's neither for or against."

Green eyes peeked over the top like a crocodile.

"It's just *about*."

"Neither *nor*," I said. "If you want to come off as a lit nerd you should learn the lingo."

She shook a little, which I took as a giggle because her eyes were smiling as they slipped back behind the cover.

»-«

The inner sanctum of the spa was an empty white room, blue and green light dancing in wavy patterns on every surface. The sound of gurgling water, which I suppose was meant to be soothing, bubbled from some cleverly hidden speaker system.

Núr Lucas sat cross-legged on a white mat wearing what can best be described as an anti-burqaë—a single strip of dark linen tied around her head, covering her eyes like a blindfold but wrapped under her long black hair, allowing it to pour freely over smooth shoulders.

Her skin was exactly the shade of the chestnut door to my office, except her broad areolae, which were distractingly large and pinkish tan around dark, thumbprint nipples. She was sitting with her hands resting casually between her legs, covering her womanhood.

"What the hell," I said as a means of introduction.

"Mr. Oliver," began the long, bizarre, enlightening conversation.

"I want to bare myself to you completely, and trust you completely, because the job for which I need to hire you requires that I know your soul better than I know your face. Please make yourself comfortable, and talk with me."

As I squatted on the mat in front of her, she crooned:

"Ëayyan-Alláh likul shay' malakan, fa likul qitëah wa jamë…"

»–«

Núr told me of angels Who etch the weather on the sketchbook of time, make eddies swirl in cream-flooded coffee, and sweep the skins of giant stars with geysers of plasma broader than the orbit of the Earth.

She drew bright lines between the angels of natural law and those Who governed the false compartments of our imaginings, like the "Four Winds" and the houses of the Zodiac.

She explained the wispy angelettes of ephemeral events, and the servile guardians who keep the eternal covenant of the Light.

Her voice slowed as she went into the angels of sentiment, Who define our perceptions and motivations, Who echo the archangels in a fractal repetition of their numbers and arrangement, but Whose purpose is specifically focused upon civilizing the offspring of countless sentient Adams and Eves riding the evolutionary whirlwind throughout the dark and frozen reaches of Creation.

"Your beef has something to do with these angels."

I said it without even the hint of a question mark.

Blinded by the cloth, she regarded me for a moment, her head angled slightly as if she were replaying my statement in a loop.

"With the Seven Sins exactly," she nodded, "The chiefest of the angels of sentiment. One of Them in particular."

Her head tilted in thought again.

"None of this surprises you?"

"You learn to take things in stride in my business, or you don't stay in business."

The merest hint of a grin spoiled the careful calm of her full, serious lips for about four frames, before she snatched it back to where I couldn't see it.

"Even so, I'm not sure I'm your boy," I went on. "Sounds like you need an exorcist, not a detective."

"What if I told you I tried that mode?"

"What if you tell me and find out what if?"

"See? You are down to earth. You see things as solid phenomena, even metaphors, firmed up into something tangible."

"*Hardboiled* is the cliché you're looking for," I quipped. She took a deep, chest-heaving breath, and for a moment I lost my mind.

"Perhaps … I need someone who can pin this angel down, handcuffed and harmless, not someone who will quote scripture and philosophy into the ether."

Fair enough. A detective story was what she wanted.

"So, what about the Seven Sins? You mean the standards?"

"Pride, Anger, Lust, the rest. I do not know the names you learned."

"Van… Vana?" I struggled. "Which is pride. Then Ira for rage, Luxury for lust. Avarice, greed."

I stared at the ceiling and squinted as if that would squeeze the memories out through my eye sockets.

"The Latin names," she said. "Gula for gluttony, Invidia for envy, and Socordia for sloth."

"You know your stuff."

ON THE HEAD OF A PIN

I stared at the blindfold, trying to detect a motion, a mere flutter of eyelashes. Nothing moved. I doubled down on the prompt.

"You must have studied them pretty hard."

And she had. Núr filled me in on how she had studied the Sisters by playing tease to a Trappist monk in Saskatchewan, a Jewish psychotherapist in Hilo, a professor of classics in Adelaide, and a pair of Tibetan Buddhists who worked as accountants in Sheboygan Falls, Wisconsin.

Let's just say that, beyond the appeal of her physique, she was also a good cook, a wily investor, a convincing efficiency consultant, and possessed several other talents that served her spiritual experiments quite successfully.

She was scoping out the Seven Sins, using her serial male harem to learn Their habits the way a big game hunter studies his prey. She tracked them through history, both her own personal history and the grand skein of the world. She learned how Invidia had shaped our language, teaching us to spin words to denigrate and elevate; how Luxury and Ira had danced (and fought, as only twins can fight) in a punctuated rhythm of anarchy and tyranny; how Avarice had taught Vana to buy in bulk, seduce the entire population with delusions of grandeur.

"With democracy," her bottom lip folded in on itself, "we are all Caesars now."

"So," the detective in me insisted, "what's the case?"

She cleared her throat. I think I saw her chin drop slightly.

"Something the Australian mentioned in passing…"

"The professor put a kink in your studies?"

"Yes. One of the Sisters seems to be missing: an angel named Lýpe," she put an odd rounding on the *ý*, "more colloquially known as Despair."

"An eighth Deadly Sin?"

She nodded.

"Her discouraging influence had restrained Their bad behavior before She mysteriously disappeared.

I touched my chin with finger and thumb.

"So, she was the Eeyore of the clan back when They were an octet."

Seemed far-fetched, at least as far-fetched as one can get in a chat about semi-divine personalities who dabble in historical engineering like brats with an ant farm. At first, I wondered how I'd never heard of this "angel of gloom," but I quickly bowed out of the PhD's shadow. Maybe there was something to it.

It was quiet for a few moments, then Núr explained how she had confirmed this academic claim in the laboratory of her liaisons. And, her scientific approach was quite impressive.

No matter how blue the balls of her marks, no matter how many savory dishes she dumped in the rubbish bin, no matter how many lucrative investments she allowed to tank, no matter how often she withheld satisfaction to the other vices, this elusive eighth Sin refused to show Her face.

So, she was hiring me to find Lýpe.

Núr was concerned that Her disappearance meant there was something metaphysically ill with the world, and locating the vanished Sin was key to preventing some imminent, horrific Apocalypse. Or, more personally, that this missing angel might be waiting to pounce from the Darkness while Núr was occupied dispatching the other Sins on her way to *Fitrah*.

"Fitrah? Where's that?"

"In Sufism it is like," she chewed her bottom lip, "our original innocence, before our fissiparous individualism, when we were still one with God."

"It's a Muslim thing, then. So why are you chasing Catholic Sins to get there?"

She frowned on one side.

"In the account books for your business, Mr. Oliver, do you use Roman numerals?"

I said nothing, which was an answer in itself.

"You're a *Roman* Catholic using *Arabic* numerals. All ideas are merely tools. We use whatever works."

"Including a monk, a shrink, a prof, and a couple of bean counters."

"And a few others," she shrugged. "Do you feel sympathy for them?"

"They should've kept themselves out of trouble."

"As you do."

"Exactly."

At this she smiled.

"You *are* my boy," she cooed, "I am very pleased! Tell me you will take the case."

Of course, I took the case. I didn't take it because I needed the money—to pay gambling debts, or resolve a lien against my office, or some other corny hard luck story. I took it because finding a missing person is about the safest case you can take.

I know the real detective money was in sneaking photos of cheating spouses, but do you know how dangerous a cornered husband can be? Or wife, for that matter? Pissing off a known rule-breaker with a hefty divorce settlement in the balance can really come back to haunt you, and then leave you coming back to haunt.

No, C. R. Oliver Investigations excels in finding long-lost adopted siblings, locating the graves of ancestors for genealogy nuts, doing bug sweeps for the tinfoil hat crowd. Inconsequential stuff, but enough of it to keep the bills paid.

Núr's little quest to sniff out where some emo angel had been moping seemed the surest account I had ever scored.

"Where will you look first?" she asked, still sitting straight as a statue. My knees were killing me from squatting on the floor. I got to my feet, and her face followed me, leading me to suspect the opacity of that anti-burqaë. Or, maybe she heard me get up and was just aiming her face where she expected my voice.

"Well, I'll want the full names of your former," I paused, trying to set the right tone, "test subjects, in case I need to look in on them to burn off any loose threads."

She nodded slowly.

"That will be fine."

Her lips crinkled a bit. Not sure what that meant.

"But," I went on, "the best place to start looking for an absent Eighth, I figure, is among the Seven remaining."

Her mouth dropped open.

ON THE HEAD OF A PIN

"You just want to walk right up to Them?"

"Do I seem like someone who's going to fall for—"

"—one of the Seven? No."

Then, she smiled, and I've never seen a face roll so fast from night to day.

"The *audacity* of it, Mr. Oliver!"

This doll has full, dark lips and her smile was a challenge not to kiss right off her face. But, flings with clients always end badly—*always*—so I kept it business-like.

"Where do these Sisters party?" was my only question. Núr was happy enough to give me directions to Their dance club on the shadowy edge of reality.

PART TWO

The name of the place was Pressure, a bright neon sign sporting three olives, like someone had spilled a loaded martini. The cardiac rumble of EDM from deep inside the barrel-faced building, however, told me this was no martini bar.

How had I gotten there? Núr had explained how. I'll get to that later. Too early to slow down the pace with all that.

There was no one outside Pressure except a sullen little butterface vamp with hair as green as seaweed, leaning against the wall next to the double brass doors. She gave me a very skeptical elevator glance as I walked up, and didn't seem too pleased at the cranberry monkstraps I was strolling up in.

"Are you," I wasn't quite sure how this translated to the angelic context, "checking IDs?"

She served me a sour look like She wanted to eat me alive and wash it down with a tall glass of my Type O negative.

ON THE HEAD OF A PIN

"Charles Roland Oliver, I *remember* you."

I had never seen this Chick in my life and She remembers me, name and all. One of the perks of being an angel, I guess.

"So," I lifted my eyebrows, "cover fee?"

Eyes rolled and emerald lips parted for a sigh.

"Sure thing, pal."

She held out a fist, knuckles up, and unrolled Her fingers one by one. Each nail was filed to a predatory point.

"Three bucks. *In dimes*."

Obviously, She was not the bouncer.

"How about I just leave You alone and show myself in?"

"Your funeral, bub."

»–«

Light rained down on the room, like sprinklers armed with fire rather than water. The reggaeton throb of Pitbull's *Infierno* shook the floor like a liquid. A crowded bar stretched down the left side, forming a right-angle with a DJ table in the back, a gamma defining the circulation of the dance floor.

> TU CORAZÓN LATE, BABE-E-E-E-EH
>   DON'CHA KNOW IT, WHERE YOU ARE?
> A TÍ NO TE PUEDE-E-E-E-ES
>   RESPIRAR O PENSAR
> BIENVENIDO AL INFIERNO!
>   TORTURADA POR TU DESEO
> BIENVENIDO AL INFIERNO!
>   WE GONNA DANCE 'TIL WE CAN'T DANCE
>   NOW DANCE

The DJ booth only reached halfway across the far wall, ending near the perfectly centered rear door. Café tables, lit from within by ghostly pink and turquoise glow, clustered against the right side of the room. In the gulf between the tables and the bar boiled a fierce chaos of dancing forms—angels and mortals—churning under flickers of shadow and flame.

The Sins could fill a room. Literally.

As Núr had explained and I now witnessed for myself, the Seven have spored off Daughters like Third-World Catholics, Gula Herself being particularly prolific. She is the Mother of all addictions, of the quarter million things you can buy at a Super Walmart, of knowingly risking a brain freeze while slurping a cold drink, and scratching at it until it bleeds.

Each of which, of course, has a little angel of its own.

She and Vana, during an incestuous tryst, spawned Bulimia, who could have been any one of the flimsy, dragon-chasing waifs haunting the club that night, and insulting the female form. Gula had once even rubbed against the Likeness Itself, giving birth to Curiosity, Who happened to be the first friendly smile I saw as I crashed the party.

A moment after I stepped through the double brass doors into the insane heat of the Sister's clubhouse, Curiosity locked eyes on me from across the lake of flushed and fevered dancers, sparked a sly grin that led me wrongly to guess that She was Mischief, and weaved Her way toward me through the writhing, grinding flesh.

Being a more derivative angel, Curiosity wore the image of youth, bouncy blonde curls swirling around a warm, round face that glittered under the flashing lights of the dance hall. Her slim hips betrayed only the barest hint of swaying to the beat vibrating from every wall.

Her Mother and Aunts, on the other hand, hovered near the far turntables like cougars, ancient gazes sweeping the dance floor seeking out new playthings.

Luxury (I guessed) was thrusting aggressively to the rhythm, red curls tossed back and forth. Militant in a burgundy pants suit, Ira (I deduced) was yelling at someone for leaning against the sound system, while Gula (I assumed) was tending the bar nearby, wearing little more than a lemon yellow bra and God-knew-what, if anything, down below.

"You're looking for something," Curiosity shouted over the thump, right before we introduced ourselves. "I am Curiosity."

"Charles Oliver," I said, "But You probably already knew that."

"Oliver? Is that the Latin or the Germanic version?"

I had no idea what the hell She was talking about.

"I'm just happy to see a smiling face. The Green Girl outside was giving me a *wicked* stink eye."

Her hand covered a smile.

"That was Misfortune. We don't let Her in the club for a reason."

She giggled, grabbed my arm, and dragged me into the bouncing mélange of angels and mortals.

"Let's dance."

The hints of rhythm in Her body became more explicit as She slipped a thigh between my legs, thus requiring one of mine to slip between Hers.

Although I am not a cat, I was a bit intimidated to be dancing with Curiosity, especially when Her emotive namesake dug its claws into my brain as firm angelic breasts were pressed against me.

Curiosity let Her cheek touch mine. Her skin was shockingly warm.

"What are you looking for, Mr. Oliver?"
"Your Aunt Lýpe," I said, approximating Núr's pronunciation as closely as I could. It came out sounding more like "Loopy."

She pulled back and dealt me a frisky grin. The overhead lasers sprinkled red and green stars across Her face.

"Lýpe doesn't come to Our parties anymore," She shouted across the new distance between Her lips and my ear.

Giving in to the intrigue, I pulled Her back to intimate contact. She was chewing Her bottom lip as She disappeared beside my face. Her womanhood made purposeful contact with my thigh—the heat was inhuman, almost painful.

"My client noticed She's missing. I'm just trying to find out why."

"Your client?"

"Núr Lucas."

"Also an interesting name!"

She leaned back, but intensified the pelvic pressure, grinding as the beat backed out of reggaeton into some Calderone trance remix. When She leaned forward again, She moved in close and cocked Her head to one side.

"It's too bad angels don't have true names. You could use it to find Her."

"What do You mean?"

"You have a true name, but you don't know it. Every little dross has a true name, because *you're* specific."

I was confused and She could tell.

"Roughly speaking," She said with teasingly lowered lids, "you have a relative locus of perception in spacetime. That's your true name, your personal identifying nomenclature."

Glancing across the steaming crowd, I noticed we were being scrutinized sharply by a Sister in a red-brown dress. Invidia? I closed the already meager distance between Curiosity's face and mine.

"And You don't have a true name?"

"No, silly. We're *archetypal*." On the letter P, She puffed out Her lip, almost brushing mine. "Angels exist wherever We're expressed."

There was a flicker of that mischievous grin again, then She looked innocently up into the spinning lights, lips pursed in thought.

"Well, except for the guardian angels, but they don't really have their own true names so much as they just use the pin of the creature to which they were assigned."

Pin?

Before I could ask what She meant by "pin" my eye caught the wicked glare of that Sister in the bay-colored dress again. The ferocity of Her vigilance was making my blood itch.

Curiosity followed my line of sight, tossing a glance over Her shoulder. Grabbing my hips but still facing the Sisters, She rocked back and forth with the beat, like She was showing me off.

Then She laughed, the Sister in the bay dress shrugged, and I was suddenly looking into that cute round face again.

"That was My Mama, Gula, stomping Her hooves at you."

Ah, so I was wrong assuming the bartender was Gula.

"So, Who's handing out drinks?"

"Oh, that's Avarice, and She's not *handing out* anything. You'd be shocked at what She's charging for just a ginger ale."

Curiosity nodded again toward Gula.

"Mama was just worried that you're too disciplined to entertain Me, but We'll see about that."

She leaned in, the corner of Her mouth touching mine as She slid Her cheek against my face. For a moment, I wondered how the fullness of those lips would feel against mine. Or against my tongue.

I regained my senses.

"You said a *pin?*"

The resulting giggle made Her chest shake against me.

"How to locate anyone mortal and specific. We call it the Personal Identifying Nomenclature now, instead of *true name*. Like your debit card codes. P, I, N, *PIN*."

Then She whispered, Her lips brushing my ear, "because We think it's funny."

In a flash, my mind was burning with intense interest. Imagine what a detective like myself could do with this ultimate locator, like some cosmic GPS. Quite a neat little tool!

"You know their PIN and you can find anyone?"

"Any-*one*, any-*thing*," She said, as if to remind me that we were all pretty much objects to Them.

Then, Curiosity told me something that slipped past scorching sexual hunger *and* the ambition to rule my professional kingdom, burying itself like a grappling hook in my mortal psyche.

"But, you brainy little creatures who can *know* things, you're trrrrrouble."

She leaned back, squinting at me mischievously, biting Her lip, thrusting Herself against me in a cloth-frustrated simulation of coitus.

"Because, if you figure out your PIN, you can *change* it," a hard thrust, leaning closer.

"And then We'd *never*," even closer, eyes fixed on mine.

"Be *able*," noses touching, eyes closing.

"To *catch* you."

»–«

Of course, They didn't really call it a PIN, because angels don't have Their own language, despite what Medieval mystics would have you believe. A lot of that "angelic language" nonsense was a joke of Theirs at the expense of the credulous and overly ambitious.

Have you seen some of the convoluted symbols in that so-called language? I can imagine Curiosity giggling at that.

No, language is for the meat-bound, not for Those who only dress up in flesh to play around. God only knows how angels communicate ideas like "true names" among Themselves. They certainly don't refer to them as PINs. Curiosity was just messing with me, in Her way.

Well, in *one* of Her ways. Later, She and I messed around in another of Her ways in Her room upstairs, repeating our dance without so much interfering cloth, but with a technopop bass still pounding out a guiding rhythm from the dance hall below.

After I had satisfied my curiosity (and my Curiosity) She propped Herself up on one shoulder and asked if I would like to trade places.

Trade places? "You mean, with You on top?"

"That *could* be part of it, yeah." She waggled Her head.

Oh. That.

She giggled. "Don't be such a prude. I'm already inside you, in a sense, being an angel of affect. We'd just be making the physical reality mirror the spiritual."

She leaned over, cupped my pecs, and licked the left half of Her grinning upper lip.

"On Earth as it is in Heaven, so to speak."

"Maybe next time, Doll." Definitely not next time.

But, despite my show of resistance, Curiosity (and the uncapitalized namesake She ruled) had gotten under my skin. The idea of a true name by which you could immediately locate something no matter where in Creation it was, a sort of detective's cheat code, spun around and around in my head until it got turned inside out.

If knowing my own true name meant I could change it at will and They'd never be able to find me ... well, *They* would include Death and all sorts of lesser calamities.

To think, I could set aside my mortality as easily as setting aside a cup of booze. Forget America's Safe New World. I could live in a Safe New Universe.

"What's gotten into you, handsome?" Curiosity smirked and leveled Her eyes at me. "If not me?"

"I was just—" I stopped short, realizing She was jilling Herself under the sheet. She grinned full-on at my recognition. Relentless.

"I love you more than the Others do," She said, arm moving like a piston. I must have looked surprised, because She laughed and slowed down. But didn't stop.

"I love you *plural*. You brainy types."

Her rhythm slowly picked up, Her breath catching.

"So few of you dross—you *animals* are curious, I—I mean, as the core of what you are—oh—curious for its own sake—and not just to fill an—appetite…"

My body was taut, urging me to join Her. I slipped a knee over the closer of Her legs, and She responded by easing them wider.

She looked me in the eye, panting, mouth loose.

"Any—clump of cells can get angry or—lusty."

Eyes closed, back arched. I could feel Her hand, knuckles rigid, moving furiously against my thigh as I slowly leaned over Her.

"They all love to play with my Aunts, Charles—Charles! But *your* kind loves Me for Me."

She shuddered like She was sobbing.

"With you I am free of Them!"

Curiosity bolted suddenly, chest slamming hard against mine, legs clamped tight. I hooked my arm around Her waist and held Her there as She shook.

She was as hot as a barber's towel. Steam poured from Her skin, hair. Arms swept around my shoulders, clawing, Her face weeping against my neck. Slowly, She settled into shivers.

Her Aunts. God, I still had to walk out past the Sins, seven of the least lesser calamities. Curiosity might be free of Them with me, but I sure as hell wasn't.

My carnal urgency vanished like a popped bubble, replaced by an urgency of purpose. Núr's little mystery of the lost angel could wait. I needed to find a way to discover my PIN first. But how?

Well, if everything has its angel (as Núr claimed) I figured that somewhere there had to be Someone in charge of giving people the answers to questions. After all, Chuck Oliver had conceived of it even while distracted by the sun-like heat of Curiosity's steaming wet skin, and God's Imagination must be far more thorough and focused than mine.

Absolutely so, even an amateur theologian might reasonably assume.

Curiosity tossed Her arms wide and collapsed, grinning and giggling, tears fossing into the gold, sweat-darkened hair on either side of Her gorgeous face.

"It's so nice," the angel laughed, brushing my chest weakly with one hand, "to be with a guy who indulges Me."

I put my lips on Her cheek, and She mmmed, pushing back against my kiss with the dimple of Her smile.

As I indulged Her post-coital playfulness, however, I was hesitant to ask Curiosity where I could find the angel of Response, or whatever Her name might be. A gentleman doesn't ask a girl about another girl while still in the first girl's bed. Even if that girl is a Girl. Plus, Curiosity and Response would likely work at cross-purposes, if basic semantics held any sway.

Then again, Response might satisfy Curiosity far better than I could. So maybe They were BFF's?

"Come on, Charles. What are you thinking about now?" She purred.

A single fingernail traced my shoulder. Her eyes were filled with Herself. Or maybe suspicion.

Yeah. Not worth the gamble, I decided. Time to head back to Núr's place to ask for more directions.

"Just that I should get back on the case," I excused myself. "My *professional* curiosity calls, but I'll be back to see You, love."

With that vague promise, I slipped my clothes on, and made my way downstairs.

When I got down to the dance hall, there was apparently some sort of intermission going on, angels and dross mingling on the floor, Gula tapping through a playlist on the mixer screen.

Vana was leaning against the wall in Her gold dress, arms folded over breasts, ankles crossed, and one eyebrow cocked. She tucked the tip of Her tongue into the corner of Her lips and let out a burst of air.

"Well, well ... here's the man himself!"

I wasn't sure it would be a good idea to just blow by an angel who was clearly not pleased with me, especially one of the Sisters whose Niece I had just thumped the hot nethers with, so I stopped.

Luxury leaned over Vana's shoulder, one red curl falling over Her fierce, dark eyes.

"Whataya want, hot shot? A crown?"

The heat from Her voice was like a furnace.
Avarice snorted from behind the bar, "She should go back to dating crooks."

Socordia, washing Her hands at the sink beside Avarice, snickered and shook Her head. This was not good. I decided to make a show of being properly humiliated and then ease my way out through the crowd.

But, Curiosity's mama Gula stepped in the way with Her lips pursed, looking me up and down. An elephant tusk pendant, hollow at the base like a horn, rested in ivory contrast to the sienna of Her chest.

She blew one black spiral of hair off Her forehead, reached out, grabbed my wrist, and pulled it toward Her. With a velvet-covered cylinder, She stamped the back of my hand, leaving a purple flowing pattern.

Invidia leaned in, dangling keys attached to a stick.

"Why not just give the little prince free run of the place?"

Gula shot Her an angry eye, then held my hand up to show me the stamp. Head cocked in skepticism, She asked:

"You gonna earn this?"

"If You say."

»–«

I stepped out the doors expecting to see Misfortune's snarl, like green icing on the angry cupcake the Sisters had fed me. In Her place was Ira, leaning against the sandstone cladding beside the marble door frame. She was staring into the empty street, breath throbbing in somewhat less than a seething rhythm under Her blood-toned jacket.

"I ran Her off," Ira said without turning, "if you are looking for the little Witch."

"Just heading home," I shrugged, then felt stupid for shrugging.

The angel just kept glaring at the street, eyes like pools of quiet menace, chest rising and falling like the magma chamber of a super-volcano considering whether to bury the world in smothering ash. I couldn't bring myself to step away, or even look away. It felt like there was a cherry pit stuck in my throat. I tried to swallow it, and it stung as if someone were pushing a fingernail into my carotid.

She turned Her face to me, and my skin twitched under the searing burn of a space heater way too close to my face. My eyes were dry faster than I could close them. Then they were watering so hard that tears rolled over the edge of each lid and tumbled onto my cheeks before evaporating.

I blinked and tried to start breathing again. I hadn't realized I had stopped.

Something happened in Her eyes, a decision of some kind, and She started breathing again, too. The heat dialed back a bit, and I sniffled and cleared my throat. The corner of Her mouth twitched like She was suppressing a painful grin.

She looked out into the street again.

"Do you remember when you decided to become a detective?"

With a single smooth movement, She lifted a hand to Her breast pocket, slipped two fingers in, and eased out a cigarette. Looking at me sideways, Her eyes smiled, and the tip of the cigarette caught fire in a burst of smoke.

She let Her whole face smile then, and blew out the flame. Repeating the question with Her eyebrows, She put the cigarette gently between Her lips and drew on it. The fresh-lit tobacco smell calmed me a bit.

"I guess after college," I started, "when I realized my degree was—"

"No!"

She jerked the cigarette out of Her mouth, and sparks fountained from the burning end. Her eyes flashed Herself and the heat from Her body threatened to curl my eyelashes.

ON THE HEAD OF A PIN

"*Think* for fuck's sake! *Before* that. You were just a boy."

A burst of cold washed through my body, and I shivered despite the scalding bath of infrared from Ira's presence. I could feel my lips chapping.

"I don't ... was it vigilance?"

She closed her seething eyes. When I was just a boy, think, think.

"From having to look over my shoulder every fifteen seconds?"

I licked my lips and ground my teeth.

"Because some hillbilly punk might be winding up to fling a rock into my skull?"

She wasn't moving so I thought about it. The constant threat of random, meaningless, unpunished violence I endured as a child. I had no choice to be constantly on the look-out.

The more I thought about it, the angrier I got, and Ira's scorching heat began to feel like home. I thought I smelled a fireplace, or maybe the scent of sage rising from Her skin. I suddenly wanted to put my tongue on the side of Her strong, elegant neck, taste the skin and feel the muscle respond as I closed my lips against it, even if the heat consumed me whole. It was erotic and comforting at once.

And terrifying.

"Sorry, so sorry," She hissed, and the sunfire eased off again. I settled on my heels and found myself breathing hard. She shook Her head, and a single lock of bronze hair came loose to hang over Her cheek. The rims of Her irises flickered red and orange, like twin eclipses.

"Christ, but you creatures love to trip over the categorical."

I stood there, dumb. It seemed like the best option at the time.

"The categorical. *Demographics*, Charles. Poor little white trash Charles and the poor white trash things he had to suffer."

She rolled her eyes and took a puff from the cigarette.

"If that were the case, if that were the explanation for why you became a detective, every wimpy kid in your home town would be bonded and licensed and soft-shoeing it around the big city asking all the wrong questions."

Good point. I wasn't the only picked-on kid in BFE. Self-centered mistake.

She drew hard on the cigarette and blew out a torrent of smoke into the street, like a dragon trying to boil away a pestering knight. Or a gnat. The silent consonants at the nose of both of those words struck me as funny. Or maybe I was just giddy from fear.

"Then again, maybe you are not much of a detective, either."

She ground Her teeth on the ambiguity.

"No, of course you are. But you stay buried under polite nonsense."

"I wasn't trying to be."

"Shut up!" She roared like a blast furnace.

She took a couple of deep breaths, and side-eyed me: "Wise-cracking is an affectation. Get to the essence of it. Get to when you realized you could help people by figuring things out that they could not."

ON THE HEAD OF A PIN

"I am sure I don't remember."

She waggled Her head, accepting it.

"You were a boy, on your thirteenth birthday, at the Branchtown Mall, and a woman named Anna Ashley O'Fenua was trying to find somewhere to throw away an empty grape juice bottle."

What the hell? I had completely forgotten about that, but it started solidifying in my mind like a film coming into focus.

"Yeah. Yeah? I thought it was some kind of tropical, coconut punch something."

"Not important," She puffed on the cigarette, "but it was grape juice. And a bag of almonds."

Her certainty was feeding mine: "The trash can was hidden behind this thick column. Like a square support pillar. I saw the shadow of the trash can rim on the floor beside—"

"No."

Ira took a deep, frustrated breath.

"She asked you if you knew where the trash was, and as you were looking around you saw a bird fly out from behind the column. You had not seen it fly in on the other side of the column, so you knew there was probably something there behind it."

She turned and leaned toward me. She licked Her lips, once and quickly, business-like, as if simply to wet them. Her tongue was the most pure, primary red I think I have ever seen.

"Then—*only then*—you looked for a shadow, to confirm."

Her eyes were uncomfortably steady on mine.

"I had no idea." It was the only thing to say.

"There are lots of things about yourself you do not know."

She turned away, leaned against the wall, sucked on the cigarette, looked back into the street, and smiled to Herself.

"But, I like you, because you know what you want."

"You're awfully sure," I said carefully.

"I'm also sure you won't like it when you get it."

She huffed enigmatically.

"Now get back to your Safe New World, Charles Roland Oliver."

It felt like a giant finger lifted off my chest and I could breathe again, move again. I stepped off into the street, into the cold, where there was comfort from the memory of the hot glare of Ira's conviction.

I struggled not to shiver, but failed. It was a pleasant shiver. Get back to my Safe New World? Never safe until the Sins and all the choirs of Hell could not catch me.

I must find my PIN, and change it.

I looked over my shoulder to see Ira's red-suited curves replaced by a column of cherry fire, dark and hot, little flames scratching at the wall of Pressure like fingernails.

No Safe New World that has such angels in it.

ON THE HEAD OF A PIN

ACT II

PART THREE

Now, at this point, you might be tempted to say: Come on, Chuck, is this a fantasy story or an autobiographical essay dressed up in pulp narrative and schlocky metaphor?

Look at your own life, sister. (I'm assuming you're a broad, since most readers are these days. But, maybe not.) Don't you prefer dressing up *your* life in symbols and imagery and romantic role-playing, with the same enthusiasm you dressed up dolls when you were a kid and pretended they were in True Love?

Or at least how you pretended they were in some serious, plastic lip-smushing Like?

I'm betting the dipshits who actually fill your daily life are unworthy of page space in any decent story, without the psychically charged roles you cast for them. *You* make them better than they are by weaving a cinematic veil of romance and adventure and symbolism around them.

Yeah, that might sound like flattery, but don't forget: *you're* the dipshit in *their* stories.

As Curiosity would phrase it, you'd much rather dance with angels than with dross, wouldn't you? You strike through the pasteboard mask of material reality (and, in the process, punch your little guardian angels in the chops) in order to get to the delicious, nourishing spiritual archetypes underneath.

Nom-nom-nom.

It makes life worth living and, paradoxically, it makes life more "true" even as it flirts with lies.

And, for a detective, digging through these pedestrian half-truths really matters, so long as you're not in some Old World, jigsaw-puzzle cozy mystery where the suspects and victims really are nothing but types.

You listening, Professor Plum?

For a hardboiled detective like me, what solves a mystery—including the mystery of your daily life—is finding the murderer, the target, the grifter, the kidnapper, the mark *beyond* all the noise of gritty, distracting, dipshit reality.

Sure, a missing Person like Lýpe might be a wonderful Aunt (or even a Mom, who knows?) with scads of interests and motives and quirky idiosyncrasies, but what mattered to me under all that was the archetypal role She took on when She went missing.

That is, it *would* matter to me if I hadn't put off trying to find Despair so I could learn how to cheat Death. I don't even want to think about what role that cast me in.

»–«

I normally would not shove my client's case to the back burner for personal gain, but this PIN was too intriguing to ignore. It did make me feel like a rat to ask for Núr's help. But, I rationalized, the undetectable detective I would become had to be a better bargain for her than the mere mortal C. R. Oliver she originally hired.

The "CLOSED" sign on the spa echoed my internal conclusion. I knocked on the glass door.

Núr was dressed when she answered the door this time, but only barely, wearing a sun dress with flowers and animal designs all over it. It was after hours, so the little literary hostess must have hopped off to whatever pond she called home.

I noticed the rain stick was gone. Did it belong to the hostess?

"Mr. Oliver? Nice to see your face."

She smiled and waved me inside.

"Nice to see all of yours, for the first time."

She looked confused, then smiled a heart-snaring smile and lifted her hand to her face.

"Ah, the blindfold."

I nodded, then got to business.

"I have some leads."

I stepped past her toward the meditation room, "but I need to know how to find another angel. A specific angel."

"Your back is bleeding!"

She tugged at my shirt collar, reached around to unbutton the top button.

I turned my shoulder to look at my back in the waiting room mirror, three lines of red on the left and four on the right, courtesy of Curiosity. I grabbed the shirt front, straightened it.

"Just scratches."

"Scratches?"

"Fingernails."

Núr stepped in front of me with a stern face.

"Mr. Oliver, I am not paying you to cavort with the Fallen."

"You know how They are, Ms. Lucas. You have to play the games They understand."

"Maybe you are not the right man for the job," she shook her head and looked into my eyes, angry and blinking. "Who was it?"

"Curiosity. Hardly a Sin."

She glared at me from the tops of her eyes.

"She might have seemed like a … a *harmless pixie* to you, Mr. Oliver, but She engenders mayhem! Did She get you to do anything you normally would not?"

"She tried," I shrugged.

Núr was visibly unsatisfied with that answer.

"She wanted to 'trade places,' so to speak."

Núr cocked her head, then suppressed a chuckle, held out two fingers and flipped them.

"You mean, She and you, He and you—"

"Exactly."

"And?"

"And, I bounced a rain check."

I watched her brows teeter-totter while she reconciled the two clichés. Finally, she surrendered a one-sided smile and said, "Okay, not bad, Mr. Oliver. Send a detective under the Veil and I guess Curiosity would take an interest. She has tempted untold souls to their deaths, so do not underestimate Her."

Núr noticed the stamp on my hand. She grabbed it, held the purple swoosh up to her face, inspected it. I think she even sniffed it.

"Which one of Them gave you the stamp?"

"Curiosity's Ma— Gluttony."

I pulled my hand back. Núr touched her chin and frowned.

"Is this bad?" I asked. "It's just a hand-stamp, right?"

"Mr. Oliver..."

She looked like I just asked for a cookie two minutes after she'd already told me No.

"The Mother of an angel with whom you ... whatever you did ..."

She turned—hand waving, eyes rolling—and walked toward the meditation room. Over her shoulder, she finished the thought:

"One of the Seven, no less, has essentially invited you to come back whenever you please."

I followed her. She took a shoulder-width stance in the middle of the room facing the back, then smoothly spiraled downward into a cross-legged position like a screw embedding itself in the floor. I leaned against the door jamb, impressed with the maneuver.

"Clearly, She wants to saddle you with Her own designs. That would be trouble, yes, Mr. Oliver?"

Come to think of it, that really could be trouble. Worse trouble than the other six Sisters being snippy with me. Núr sat impassively staring at the wall, clothing the only difference from the way she was sitting when we first met.

"It could sabotage your investigation, having Gula trying to corral you into whatever it is She has in mind. Only bad can come of it."

Núr had more than made her point; now she was just rubbing it in.

"You need to undo your 'bounced rain check' with Curiosity. Call it off. Completely and abruptly."

Cripes! Did this dame want me to *find* an angel, or get trampled by one? I can't even imagine Gula's reaction if I spurned Her bouncy, blonde little filly. On the other hand, Núr was right: toying with a Mama angel's expectations was a dangerous game to play. Either way, it was ...

Hopeless.

Oh, what a wily tomato was my client. Núr was playing me, pushing me toward despair, and thus Despair. Fair enough, considering that's what she hired me for, but I had no intention of becoming the latest of her experiments in vice and virtue, another dope in her male harem of dopes.

Even so, being reminded that I had a contract to honor put the ethical kibosh on using her to help me find my PIN. The ratty feeling was too much, even if Núr would benefit in the end. I would have to locate the angel of Response myself, and the only place I knew to start looking was back at the club.

>>-<<

Coming out of the angelic context is a simple thing, like waking from a dream. You either come to because the scene has run its course, or you get shocked awake.

Going in, however, is a matter of *breaking your mind*.

That was Núr's phrase, not mine. But, unlike the phrase, you can't crib the method. Everyone's mind is different, so everyone has to break it in their own way.

Like, when you contemplate your navel and realize that this tiny, necessary scar once connected you to another life, who was similarly corded to a life before her, reaching back and so on and further along a dim road of matriarchs, beyond the Stone Age, beyond when apes stood upright, ducking under the wrath of Chicxulub, to that archaic placental Eve—skittering like a rat under the shadow of dragons—who, in lieu of laying eggs, first brought umbilical violence to birth.

Consider that long train of creatures, life directly connected to life, and the self is thrown down, made vanishingly small, and one is suddenly the mere tip end of an unimaginably long and ancient creature, with a million ribs for a million Eves, the head of a megamillenial caterpillar, nibbling at the silky veil of Plato's cocoon to see what's on the Other Side.

ON THE HEAD OF A PIN

That was how I had broken my mind, but I wasn't expecting to grow butterfly wings for the cocooned caterpillar of my maternal family tree.

I did, however, collect a sport jacket from my coatrack at the office, to cover Curiosity's lashes. It was a light tweed, little cross-threads of purple, blue, and crimson creating a plum effect over a basic weave of white.

Glancing at my desk, I considered packing a rod, but shrugged it off. My reply to Núr's inquiry was still at the top of my email queue; no new messages.

It started to drizzle as I locked up the office to head back to Pressure, and I hoped it wasn't raining there as well. Whatever "there" meant in that context.

I was thinking about my button-gazing, proud of myself for the house of metaphorical cards I had stacked up. It was a lot more impressive, I decided, this navel-chain of maternity plumbing the murky depths of the Jurassic, than the Church's hand-to-head line-up of Fathers wading into the shallow end of the genetic pool of history.

I was grounded in the material, rooted against the raging winds of the spirit. I straightened the lapels of the sport jacket a little, certain that I could face Ira or Whomever was waiting to greet me.

It was not raining in front of Pressure, and seemed far too warm for the season. The bass thumped a disco bounce as I stepped with a purpose up to Pressure's front entrance, shoes clip-clopping like a metronome on the dry pavement. I found my step inadvertently synching with the beat that leaked from the club.

I looked down at my feet, as if they were conspiring against me and, when I looked back up, I saw that Misfortune was there again, leaning against the wall in all Her green and caustic glory.

This time, however, She stepped off and slipped Herself between me and the door. Her smirk set off my warning buzzers.

"If I'd known Queen Ira was going to let you slip away, I wouldn't have been so quick to run off."

"Unlike some people," I smiled and flashed Gula's stamp, "I'm actually wanted inside."

"How precious," she sneered. "Vana give you that, Golden Boy?"

I tried to edge around Her, but She was quick, and I found myself obstructed again. Glancing down out of sheer male instinct, I noticed Her nipples were pushing against the thin cloth of Her camouflage tee. I had no idea what this Chick was excited about, but I knew it had to be bad news.

"Didn't find what you were looking for last time, Chuck?"

"It could've been worse."

I tried to ease around Her again. She put a hand on my waist and locked eyes with me.

"Could've been worse *how*?"

The moment I thought it, it happened.

Pressure evaporated and I fell hard, flat on my face onto wet concrete, my clothes inexplicably gone. The rain was freezing. It was dark, but there was some light from a nearby street lamp.

I got to my hands and knees and looked around. No clothes. No wallet. No cell phone. I had nothing but the wavy purple sigil Gula had stamped onto my hand.

ON THE HEAD OF A PIN

The street sign told me I was on the corner of Dogwood and Pine. There was the Christian bookstore and, three doors down, C. R. Oliver Investigations. X marked the spot.

It might seem less than Misfortunate to get bounced all the way back to your own block, but Lobany Place is no neighborhood to be caught roaming naked through the streets in the middle of the night. I needed to get inside quick.

I looked around again. No keys, either. Couldn't go through the main door, and I didn't want to smash the front window. Had to go through the back.

I got to my feet and rushed around the bookstore, trying not to step on anything sharp with my bare skin, and covering myself two-handed the way Núr had covered herself when we first met.

My God, why was the rain so damned cold?

The alley behind the row was in total shadow. Good for not being seen. I slipped into the dark, hoping I didn't find a couple of thieves waiting to ...

Waiting to what? Rob me?

I stumbled to a stop. There *were* two guys there, older teenagers, barely visible in the half-light peeking around the corner from the street, leaning out of the rain under the back eave of the bookstore. I immediately recognized one of them as a cashier.

They had two reactions. First, the redhead yanked his hand away from the blond, the blond thrusting what had been his only free hand stiffly down at his side. Then, they both noticed my inappropriate attire.

"What the fuck?" said the blond, appropriately.

"I was mugged," I blurted, before they got the wrong idea. It occurred to me that "mugged" wasn't exactly the right idea, but it was close enough.

The redhead reached out, then looked at his hand and pulled it back, saying: "Are you okay? Oh my God, please don't say anything!"

It took me a moment to get the whole picture, standing there, shuffling my hands to make sure I was still covered. The smoky sweet scent of marijuana filtered through the icy rain. The joint would now be hidden beside the blond's thigh. And, they'd been holding hands before red yanked his free.

Holding hands behind the Christian bookstore. Where he worked. Where they still were, together, long after closing time.

"If you don't say anything about *this*," I looked down at my naked, shivering, soaked body, "I won't say—"

"No, seriously! I can't lose this job, and my dad would go—"

"Fuck your dad," the blond said definitively, "Fucking homophobe."

Finding courage in the profanity, he swung the reefer up to his mouth and took a long drag. He sneered and tried to stare me down.

"Look, that's *their* peeve, not mine," I said, nodding at the store.

They shared a look, deciding whether to believe me.

"Do you have a crowbar or something I can get into my place with? The detective office down the block is mine."

"Um," the redhead glanced back and forth between Blondie and me. "Do we? I don't know." He pulled a key from his pocket and started fumbling with the door.

"Fuck this guy, too," the blond said and turned, jabbing the spliff at my face: "How d'we know you're the right guy?"

I tried to say something, but my teeth clattered together, and I clamped my jaw shut to stop it. The shiver didn't like being boxed in, and it fled down my spine like a watergunned cat.

"I've seen him around," Red pleaded. "You saw him the other day when we walked down to Starbucks. Charles something."

"Maybe," he coughed and squinted at me like I was a complete social degenerate. Granted, I was roaming the alleyways of Lobany Place buck-naked in a thunderstorm, but I was sick of his reactionary contempt.

"Look, you little fuckwit, I'm not in the mood for a glare down from a little punk like you."

Red flipped the joint at my head and missed. He took a step forward with one fist balled up at his side.

"Don't pull that gay-bashing shit on me while you're standing there holding your nuts. I'll beat your bigot breeder face in!"

I laughed and puffed water off my lips.

"You think I give a shit about that? I'm not religious and this is the 21st Century. Update the chips on your shoulder."

Blond just stood there, still trying to stare me down. Clearly, I wasn't getting any help here. I looked at Red, who wasn't getting anywhere with the keys. He shrugged apologetically and tried to steady his hand by pressing the knuckles against the lock and his thumb against the latch.

"Thanks, kid, but never mind." I shook my head. "Your boyfriend is an asshole. You can do better."

I started off down the alley. That wasn't enough, I decided. I stopped and turned back to Red.

"And, if you ever do better and he tries to tell your boss or your dad before you're ready, I have a seat for you in my office. We'll make sure it wasn't worth his while."

I gave blondie a mean-business look.

With that, I plunged into the darkness.

»-«

By the irregular pulse of lightning, I made my way to the rear of the detective agency. The door was pretty solid, probably not a good idea to try bashing it down. There was a small four-pane window, high up.

I tried to balance on a garbage bin, but the lid was too wet and slick. Couldn't even keep a knee on it. I was going to break my damned neck.

I spied the mud mat by the rear door, flopped it on top of the lid, and squared it off. The rubber sole held, so I carefully stepped up, shivering from the chill. I peered through the window to figure out how to lower myself down inside, and was suddenly glad I never bothered buying an alarm system.

I nearly shivered myself off the bin, regained my balance. This was the moment of truth. I set my thumbs against the wooden cross-beams of the window. If I pushed steadily and evenly, I figured, I could crack the glass and slip it from the frames.

Harder. *Harder.*

It snapped suddenly, the panes shattered, and my hands felt like fire.

I didn't bother looking at the gashes. Didn't matter. I had to get inside. Out of the cold and the rain. Ignoring the pain, I lifted myself into the window frame and dropped on the other side. Right onto the glass-studded cross-beams.

I leaned against the wall, picked the shards from my feet where I could find them in the dark, then stumbled into the bathroom and flipped on the light.

There was blood all over the floor, and me.

I yanked the first-aid kit from under the sink and wrapped my feet and hands tight. It's no simple trick to apply pressure to both feet and both hands simultaneously, but I somehow managed to slow the bleeding.

Lesson learned. Misfortune was not to be played with. No touchy.

I dried off, tucked a towel around my waist and shuffled into the office to find some clothes by the light of the computer screen.

My email inbox was flashing.

From: nurlucas256

Subject: "Why are your clothes (and things) at the spa?"

My hands were still shaking from the cold and the pain, but I typed out a quick reply, hoping Núr was still at her computer. Something

something Misfortune, something something bleeding, something something bring my stuff?

I barely had time to notice that I had fumbled half the words in the subject line before she responded that she would be right there, meaning right here.

I leaned back in the chair. Nothing to do but wait, and think through my options.

Why was Misfortune suddenly on my case, no pun intended? Why had Gula been so accommodating? Why did Ira give a damn about why I became a detective?

My hands were on the keyboard before I realized I had made a decision. I carefully tapped out a name, followed by "professor Adelaide Australia."

My answer was in the very first search entry. I quickly followed it up with the other names, qualifying the searches with "Trappist monk Saskatchewan" and "psychotherapist Hilo Hawaii" and "accountant Sheboygan Wisconsin."

At the top of every page of results was an obituary.

PART FOUR

"Misfortune let you go by the first time?"

"Yeah."

I winced as Núr cleaned the wounds. She was soaked from the rainstorm, water from her dark hair dripping onto my feet as she washed them.

"In fact," I went on, "the first time She was pretty obnoxious about not wanting to have anything to do with me."

Núr chewed her lip for a moment, wiping the cuts with cotton and alcohol.

"It is very curious that She would suddenly take an interest in keeping you away from the Sisters. Misfortune allows souls to pass by because the Sins usually end up sending them back out to Her anyway."

I hadn't told her about Ira's intervention, if that's what it was.

As Núr moved to my other foot, she began shaking her head slowly.

"It is not good to have Misfortune making Herself an obstacle in our mission."

"You mean in my case."

"Yes. In our case. She comes from a very dangerous lineage."

Núr wrapped my feet in gauze and nodded toward the desk where she had stacked my clothes.

"Thanks. Can you help me with the socks? I can get the rest of it."

"Of course."

At the desk, she looked over her shoulder.

"Do you want a clean shirt?"

"Nah, it'll likely get messed up again anyway, if They're going to start playing rough."

I glanced at the hand stamp. It had survived the rain, but the squiggly lines on the outside had faded a bit. It didn't really look like a robe anymore; a single, sword-like curve endured in the center.

On that thought, I added: "Can you open the second drawer and hand me what's in there?"

She opened the drawer, gave me a troubled look, then lifted the pistol by its grip, pinching it between two fingers.

"Mr. Oliver, this will not really help you against Them, you know."

"What do you mean?"

"You can kill the *jasad*, the body They take on, but They will simply show up somewhere else, in new clothes. And against some of Them," she held the pistol out like a piece of scrap paper, "this would not help at all."

"Like ..."

"Well, if you meet the angel of Gunpowder, I would suggest not aiming a fire-arm at Him."

I considered this a moment. She seemed genuinely concerned. It was almost touching.

"Fine, but if it can get *some* of Them out of my hair even briefly, it might come in handy."

She bridged her eyebrows.

"Mr. Oliver, for your own safety."

Never argue while naked.

"Just the clothes then."

She eased socks onto bandaged feet, but I slipped the trousers under the towel myself. As I buttoned up the shirt, Curiosity's lashings still staining the back, I got back to business: "So, I need help following a lead."

Núr sighed, put her hands on her hips.

ON THE HEAD OF A PIN

"What do you need? Expenses? Bribes?"

"I need to know how to find an angel I think would be named Response."

One brow tilted like a warped floorboard.

"Answer?"

"If you say so. I have some questions that will, with any luck, help me. My case. *Our* case."

She shook her head, but then squinted long and hard in thought.

"I guess Answer *would* know where Despair went. I should have thought of that to begin with."

Her face flickered, then rolled from night to day.

"Leave it to a detective!"

Yeah, except that I hadn't thought of it that way, either. But it was a good plan. After asking this angelic know-it-all about my PIN, I could actually do the job I was hired to do. The idea of killing two birds with one seraph immediately made me feel less of a rat.

"Answer can have a funny way of appearing," she said. "Every question is different."

I carefully pushed my feet into shoes.

"What do you mean?"

"They do not *always* appear like us. Like humans. Sometimes They appear as things, places. Even situations. I sometimes suspect I have been dancing with Answer for years, but simply cannot see Him."

She gave me the side-eye.

"Or Her."

I shrugged and stuffed keys and wallet into my pockets.

"Even so, Mr. Oliver, Answer is one of the most powerful of angels, cold and aloof, not a playful and fiery type like the Sisters and Their brood. She is on the same exalted level as Power, Integrity, Death, and the Likeness."

Núr grabbed a Post-it and pen from my desk, started scribbling.

"So, you really do not want to knock on the wrong door."

She folded the note's sticky part back onto itself and handed it to me.

"An apartment number? I thought They didn't have specific locations."

Núr flashed me a suspicious eye.

"Did your girlfriend Curiosity teach you that?"

Oops, I forgot I hadn't learned that bit of spiritual lore from her.

"She's right," Núr said, "They do not have specific locations. The flats, as you might already know, are where They meet us. It is more about *our* location than Theirs. That is how I discovered Despair was missing: I looked for Her where I expected to find Her."

I reread the address.

"It's a basement apartment? If this bunch is so important, shouldn't They live in the penthouse?"

Núr cocked her head to one side.

"Mr. Oliver, the basement *is* the penthouse in a world that is inside-out."

»–«

On Núr's advice, I approached Pressure from behind. Hey, I figured if Misfortune was going to force me to break into my office from the back, it was poetic justice to avoid Her by sneaking into the back of the angelic edifice. Light from the street lamp smeared my shadow against the gray brick of the alley.

The walls on either side were lined with trash: discarded lumps of machinery; loose pipes and planks; warped crates and grease-mottled cardboard boxes; garbage cans cradling clay figurines with faded paint; bone carvings twine-lashed to frayed feathers; moldy books; crumbling scrolls; and chunks of finely detailed mosaic showing lost gods and hybrid monsters in the throes of some forgotten apocalypse.

Rats, or something like them, scurried back-and-forth in the filthy seams behind the rubbish. I couldn't catch them in the full aim of my vision, only at the dim edges of sight. The faint sound they made was less like tiny feet rustling, and more like the crackling of static all around, like I was skulking through a glitchy USB cord.

Or a frazzled neuron.

There was a sudden rush of the scurrying things, past me and out of the alley, like ropes being dragged into the street to either side. I dropped to a crouch and reached into my jacket for the pistol, but it wasn't there. The electric hiss faded behind me as the fleeing vermin cleared out.

At the end of the dark narrows ahead a black thing paced like a feral cat, whipping an absurdly long and supple tail. It had the ears of a hare, which it kept aimed in my direction at every turn. There was no sound. The black thing paused, and light from the street behind me reflected from a spider-like array of eyes.

I felt nothing as it studied me. No fear, just a hollow where my soul used to be. Then the black thing made a scratchy sound, like a little girl whispering the word "yes" very slowly as she died of influenza.

I stood up straight. Casually, the thing turned and slipped into the darkness as silent as the night sky.

After a few seconds listening to my heart beat in my ears, I realized I could hear, faintly, Gene Vincent's "Race with the Devil" bopping from the dance floor. Pressure had a back door.

I needed to slip in quietly and make my way to the elevator. Didn't want to be seen by anyone—or Anyone. I pulled the Post-it from my pocket, checked the address Núr had written, and put it back. I stepped over to the door and pushed it in.

There was a gasp, or two.

The hallway was about three meters wide, lit by threads of indirect lighting embedded in a fluted recess just above head height. The floor was a hex pattern of rose tiles. I had seen all this earlier when Curiosity had led me up to Her room.

New this time were Vana and Luxury, each with one hand on Her chest and another holding out a cigarette. They were both breathing hard and glaring at me.

Luxury shook Her head.

"What the Hell were you doing back there?"

"Close the God-damned door!" Vana barked.

I pushed the door closed.

"Sorry, I was avoiding Misfortune."

They huffed impatiently, then laughed while rolling Their eyes, at each other but clearly *about* me.

"Because you think She lives at Our front door?" Luxury sucked a quick drag and blew the smoke down the front of Her body.

"She—" I said, "Well, I guess I assumed based on what I knew."

Vana gave Lux a probing look.

"He's not quite there yet."

She crouched down and smashed the cigarette against the rose tiles until it was dead. She left it there and stood up, straightening Her gold dress at the hips.

"Nice jacket," She said, then to Her Sister: "I'm going back in. He's all Yours."

"Actually," I said, "I'm on my way somewhere." But Vana was gone down the hallway.

"Back up to Curiosity's?" Luxury snarled provocatively, holding Her cigarette poised before Her lips.

I didn't say anything. I wasn't sure I wanted the Sins knowing what I was really up to, calling on Answer, but I was absolutely sure I didn't want to feed whatever it was She felt about me and Curiosity. I decided to wait out Her cigarette with small talk.

"Can I ask You something?"

She shrugged with Her shoulders and eyebrows, and took a drag.

"Why don't You," I said, "I mean, You-*plural*—why don't You have wings?"

She grinned, Her eyes warming with something that looked suspiciously like sympathy. She stepped away from the wall, took a stand in the middle of the hallway in her ivory heels.

Pink ribbons of silk floated from behind her, weaving into each other and spreading outward to either side. There was a shiver, and the twin sheets of silk resolved themselves into a pair of softly feathered wings.

In that white dress, with her flaming red hair and pink wings, she looked like a Valentine's Day card.

"Is that what you wanted to see, sugar?"

Her wings stretched, lightly brushing the walls, and a tiny smirk tickled the corner of Her mouth.

"Not exactly what I'd prefer to spread for you."

My face was hot. I felt foolish.

"I guess You could look however You want, huh?"

"Or however *you* want."

Her eyebrows pumped once, suggestively. Glancing once at the ceiling in annoyance, She folded Her wings and lifted the cigarette to Her mouth.

"I can't figure out what you're looking for," She said, "and that probably means you've got your mind made up. But, to answer your question, it's all about what you're looking for. We're kinda stuck following your lead. That's how We dance."

She crushed the cigarette against the wall and flung it to the floor beside Vana's.

"All of us, except the Adversary and his kind."

"I don't feel like I'm in the lead here," I confessed. I tried to swallow it as it came out, but I wasn't quick enough.

She got that sympathetic look again and stepped toward me, one foot directly in front of the other. When She got to me, Her lips tightened and she buttoned the top button of my jacket.

"Muted asymmetry," She said, as if that meant something to me.

"Don't think of it as dancing. Or even angels. Open your mind a bit, until you find a way to get it."

"Asymmetry, like in physics?"

She smiled wide, and I felt a rush of comfort like coming inside a warm house from a blizzard. Her wings formed a half dome over us.

"There you go! Real asymmetry isn't the universe being dominated by matter; the real asymmetry would be if antimatter were impossible. So sure, most angels bow to your perceptions in some way. We were told to. But the Adversary and His children do not bow. They keep the order. You can't all simultaneously have your way, so They bring checks and balances. To keep it real."

I found my hands on Her waist. Her eyes made me feel like I'd been running a 50-meter dash. But it felt like the most comfortable, natural thing in the world. It felt like life itself, run through a still, bottled, and smuggled into my blood.

She fixed the next button on my jacket.

"So yeah, a lot of your trouble you bring on yourself, but some of it is brought to you. Don't let it make you feel like you've gone off the rails. You're doing fine."

"Am I? You seem awfully certain of that."

"Ha!"

She shoved me, but not hard enough to shove me away.

"I don't even know what the Hell you're up to, Chucko. I am certain of nothing, open to anything."

She shrugged with closed eyes, and pulled away, wings folded behind Her.

"That' why the Twin and I don't get along so well."

"Twin?"

She produced a cigarette from the sleeve of Her dress and considered it.

"Ira, that Beast. Brigadier General Hard-Ass."

She frowned and put the cigarette away. As if in compensation, Her wings faded into wisps of pink mist.

"But, She is loyal, I suppose."

I was glad not to have to wait out a second cigarette. I just stood there, nodding like an idiot.

She stared back. I stopped nodding. Finally, She blinked.

"Oh well, I'm out. Have fun with the Girl, now that Her Mama's given you the stamp of approval."

I glanced at the hand stamp, but not too closely. I glanced over my shoulder down the hall, toward the stairs to Curiosity's room, but regretted that too.

"I have no idea why Gula gave me that." I tried to sound nonchalant, but it seemed dangerously dismissive when I hit replay in my head.

"Good little Catholic boy," Luxury giggled. "What do you think Gluttony is? The Food Network angel? Just a gourmet Me? Just a culinary Avarice?"

She put Her hand on my chin.

"She is the desire to fortify yourself, taken to excess. Just my suspicion, but I think She likes you because you do that with information, rather than food."

She leaned in, Her face so close I could feel the heat on my cheek, Her lips next to my ear.

"And yours is a story about information isn't it? So put that morsel in your cute little mouth and roll it around on your tongue."

She leaned away with a flirty half-grin, but my face didn't make Her happy. Her mouth fell open, Her eyelids dropped, and I felt like I had been evicted from my childhood home.

"Why don't you like Me?"

She furrowed Her brows, and Her red curls writhed on Her shoulders like Medusa's serpents. A burning, magenta glow grew around Her, like a sailor's threatening sunrise. Her voice came like the howl of a gale: "You think I'm trying to seduce you?"

"I—I mean, You're—"

I averted my face from Her heat.

"Charles Roland Oliver, I am not a Whore!"

Her glow flashed nuclear, then vanished. I grimaced at the sudden cold and darkness. I wondered for a moment if I were dead. My eyes adjusted to the indirect lighting of the hallway, and I peered through it. Luxury was blinking hard.

"Not just a Whore," She said, "I hope—"

Her shoulders slumped. Her lips quivered, not quite together. She shook Her head and waved coral fingernails at me, like brushing bread crumbs off a table.

"I hope you find whatever it is you're searching for."

I wanted to apologize, but She evaporated in a streamer of fog, blowing off down the hallway after Vana, back to the dance, to easier souls.

Chuck, old salt, you're going to make enemies of every... I stopped myself and capitalized "Enemy" in my head, to drive home the point. Is this how Núr's other men met their ends?

Hold up. You are not one of Núr's men. Or are you?

Does it matter? The sooner I find my PIN and change it, the sooner I don't have to worry about any of these crazy questions.

ON THE HEAD OF A PIN

Great, a detective who doesn't like questions. What are you doing, Charles?

I pulled the Post-it from my pocket again, to confirm what I already knew. To find certainty.

Apartment number seven. That's what I'm doing. Looking for Answer, because I'm tired of questions.

Down the hall, beside the stairwell that led up to where the Sins and their offspring stayed—up where Curiosity was probably sleeping off our encounter (I flattered myself)—I located the elevator.

It was a gothic, antique-looking piece of business. The gates were ironwork, tips filed to predatory points, and they opened to reveal a car with walls of smooth, green stone.

As I rode the elevator down, down, down from what I guess was "ground level," the Richter-pegging rockabilly bass from the dance hall receded, and I obsessively rubbed the apartment number Núr had written down, as if trying to memorize it with my thumb.

Answer lived in number seven. Seven, seven, seven. Get the door right. Of all the angels on Her floor, She was definitely the only one I wanted to see.

You may have noticed the angels have all been "She."

Some have theorized that angels are androgynous, but that's not exactly right. Those who want your attention appear as what you desire or understand. (I guess that's a bit of a confession wrapped in an explanation.)

The reverse is also true: Those whose image you find repulsive or obnoxious or simply uninteresting are that way because They are just as happy with you leaving Them alone.

Luxury was right: It's all about what you're looking for.

For example, if what you're looking for is an intimate confidant then you might see Ira as a friend who gets infuriated at everyone who has ever done you wrong. If what you're looking for is, I don't know, an absentee father ... then Ira might show up as Darth Vader.

I was curious to see what Answer would look like, considering that my interest in angels had shifted significantly since the frolic with Curiosity. This PIN business was serious and personal.

When the elevator gates finally parted, the door straight ahead had a brass number zero screwed to it. That was weird, but this was an "inside-out" world, as Núr put it.

I looked to the next door on the left, and noticed a brass 3 which had obviously been spun upside-down on its screw. You'd think angels would have better building maintenance than that.

The next door to the right of apartment 0, luckily enough, was number 7. Not sure what order these apartments were in, maybe some sort of Qabbalistic sequence.

No matter. I walked down to apartment 7.

I knocked, and felt a voice in the center of my head like I was wearing ear-buds: "Just open the door."

Already, a quick Response! I twisted the knob and heard a click.

I don't remember stepping into the room or closing the door behind me. But, that is how things were when I saw Her.

ON THE HEAD OF A PIN

She was in darkness somehow—a silhouetted Figure 8 with legs—
even though the only lights in the room were to either side of the
door behind me and should have lit Her up as bright as a billboard.

However, those two lights still cast Her shadow onto the back wall
in either direction, giving the appearance of black wings shifting
on Her shoulders as She strutted purposefully toward me.

"You will not find Her here, Charles Roland Oliver."

Was She talking about Despair? That was *not* my first question,
Answer!

"You will find neither of Them here."

The light finally reached the angel after what seemed years, as if
hesitant to touch Her form, and there were clear indications that I
had come to the wrong room.

Her skin was white as a frozen river, hair black as a midnight sea.
Her eyes were the pale blue of a dry winter sky, but the 'whites' of
them were coal black. Her fingernails were little ovals of onyx,
Her lips wet licorice. She wore a silk dress that dripped from Her
curves like a coat of tar.

"Death," I said, "You're not as skinny as I thought You'd be."

That was, of course, a lie. She was, *of course*, exactly how I
thought She would be.

"I saw you leave the party with Curiosity, and I knew that a tumble
with Her would leave you determined to come looking for Suviel."

I tried to reproduce the name: "Suviel? Well, at least that sounds
like an angel's name for a change."

Death laughed, showing black pearl teeth.

"She is also known as Rumor, when secretly carousing with the Sisters. We only use Our -el names when We are behaving Ourselves. And We can only behave when *you* behave. And you, Mr. Oliver, for some reason have only just started trying to behave yourself."

"Sometimes it takes a kick in the pelotas to—"

She didn't let me finish my bullshit explanation.

"I do not want you looking for Her, Charles."

My gut told me She thought I was still looking for Despair.

"Well, I'm following my own curiosity now. Núr isn't paying me enough to hunt down this missing angel."

I immediately realized how dumb it was to admit this so glibly. Death peered at me, eyes narrowing until they were nothing but shimmering blue discs.

"Now you are misbehaving very badly, Charlie."

She seemed peeved and intrigued at once.

"Angels can only see what falls within Their demesne and, Mr. Oliver, *everything* eventually falls within My demesne."

She stopped an arm-length away and scraped my cheek with Her fingernails, thumbnail scratching my chin. They felt like ice.

"Yet, I cannot see what you are looking for, so you must be trying to find a way to cheat Me."

She took a deep breath, like a hurricane siphoning up the heat of a tropical sea.

"You are looking for your true name, are you not?"

No point in lying about it now; the Queen Bitch was within striking distance.

"Impressive. You've subtracted so many lives from the world, and yet You can still add two plus two."

"Curiosity runs Her mouth too much," She said flatly. Now I knew that finding my PIN did indeed lead to a path hidden from Death. A tasty piece of information, but not much use while I was still in the room with the emissary of my demise. I needed to get the hell out of there.

She took my bandaged hands in Hers, flipped them palms up and grinned.

"My little Girl plays rough, you think?"

Misfortune was Death's daughter? Made sense. *Dangerous lineage* indeed.

Then, Death surprised me.

"Would you like a drink?" She asked, as casual as a former lover.

Assuming my assent, She moved toward a tall liquor cabinet, red-lacquered with an Asian village scene incised and blackened on the doors.

That's the first chance I got to take a good look at Death's place. It was filled with antiques, likely souvenirs of Her favorite prizes. There were Spanish colonial chairs around an English tavern table, a Persian carpet in cream with red and blue gazelles dancing around the perimeter, a folding screen with a lot of blue people on it for some reason, and a small square table in the corner draped with a black velvet cloth.

Opening the liquor cabinet, Death looked over Her shoulder, expectantly.

"Bourbon."

"How do you take it?"

I glanced at the enduring blade of Gula's hand stamp.

"High and neat."

"You clay types," She shook Her head as She poured, "even when you have a clear template through which to understand sin, you screw it up. Do you know how many people think Gilligan is Socordia's baby?"

What the Hell was She talking about?

"Who?"

"Socordia,"

She reached back to hand me the tumbler. The ice clinked like a windchime made of human bones.

"The angel of Sloth."

I tried to smile graciously as I took the booze.

"I've met Her. I meant: Gilligan from the television show?"

Somehow, the idea of Death Herself lounging around watching reruns of *Gilligan's Island* seemed absurd to me.

"Yes hon," She sang, leaning against the cabinet and grinning at my confusion.

"Even the man who concocted the series thought that Gilligan represented Sloth. But, if you watch carefully, you will see that his weakness is not leisure."

She sipped something red but suspiciously thicker than wine from Her glass.

I stared into my bourbon, wondering offhandedly if She had poisoned it. Indeed, was Death capable of *not* poisoning a drink?

"Gilligan never gives in to Mr. Howell's money or Ginger's flirtations. The only way the castaways could get him to do anything was—"

"Coconut cream pie!" I blurted in sudden realization. I had interrupted Death's explanation, but it was only fair considering Her earlier interruption of mine. Her sly grin hinted that She agreed, or was at least pleased by my epiphany.

"So, if Gilligan was Gula's, who belonged to Sloth?"

"Mrs. Howell," She stated blankly with a roll of Her night-dark eyes. She set the glass on the cabinet behind Her.

"Like most wives of money, she was a lazy lump of shit."

Her pallid gaze softened and She moved closer. Real close.

"But none of the Seven are *your* particular vice, are they Charlie?"

Uh-oh. She had been hunting me through that conversation, and I missed it while worrying about the drink.

Of course Death used the Seven and Their progeny to draw people in—She was, as the Apostle put it, Their wage.

"You seem to like Curiosity, though."

Her dark fingernails forced their way through my hair at even intervals, like a search party sifting the woods for a murdered kid. I could feel Her breath on my neck, the frigid exhaust of an air conditioner.

"Do you realize," She whispered ice into my ear, "one kiss from Me, and you would know everything there is to know? Your soul opens to the Knower of all things, and your curiosity is utterly satisfied."

As intriguing as this bit of eschatological insight was, at that moment I didn't want to know everything there is to know. I just wanted to know *one* thing: how to get the hell away from Death.

But, I reasoned frantically, if a kiss would reveal *everything* there is to know, then maybe a near-kiss, the mere prelude to a smooch, might be enough to put an escape plan into me.

I knew that if I thought about the PIN, about trying to set Death aside forever, She would immediately detect it, like She had before. So, I purposefully resolved myself to a path that kept a deep drink of Death firmly in my future; I wanted nothing but a momentary reprieve. I could go looking for the PIN later.

Or not. Don't think about it, Chuck old boy.

One little touch for one little piece of information. With no intention of follow-through, I brushed Her cheek with my hand as if making to lock lips.

There was flash between us and a loud crack. She looked more surprised than I was, and we both glanced down. The pistol in Her hand had gone off into the meat of my side before She could raise it to my heart.

The tumbler thumped against the Persian rug and I stumbled backward with my hand just above my hip, blood spilling between my fingers. Like checking a set of cards, I hinged my hand away from the wound to look at it. Painful, but possibly survivable.

I lifted my eyes to Death, but the entire scene was already starting to dissolve. Nothing will bring you back to mundane reality like taking a bullet to the belly.

Goddamn metaphors. It put the escape plan "into" me alright.

On a crazy impulse I winked at Her as She faded.

"Very clever," Her hovering smile said. "Catch you later, Charlie."

PART FIVE

The bleeding wasn't bad, but it was still an open bullet wound, not something you just want to push against and hope it goes away. I shuffled to Núr's spa, gambling that she would still be there, chanting or spinning in circles or something.

A couple of knocks, and she came to the door in jeans and a dark orange t-shirt.

"Oh! What happened?"

She slipped her shoulder into my armpit and guided me toward the meditation room. The rain stick was leaning near the door, and I judicially avoided knocking it over as I limped along.

"Death was there. We had a little chit-chat, She poured me a drink, shot me in the gut, you know. It was a nice visit."

"Death was there?"

ON THE HEAD OF A PIN

She crinkled her nose as she helped me to the white floor mat.

"Did you go to flat number seven?"

"Am I stupid?"

Getting shot was making me snippy.

"The apartments were out of sync but the door I knocked on had a seven on it."

She opened a closet and started digging through shelves for something.

"What do you mean, out of sync?"

"Out of order. There was a three, then a zero, then a seven..."

Holding a first-aid kit in both hands, Núr cinched her brows in confusion for a moment, then rolled her eyes.

"*Suhqan!* She switched to Hindí numbers!"

"What are you talking about?"

"You went to number *six*— Take your shirt off already."

She knelt and opened the kit.

"Number *six*, but in a different number system. In Hindí numerals, the ones we use in Arabic, four looks like a backward three, five looks like zero, and six looks like seven."

"That's kinda stupid," I said. "And, I don't even *know* those numbers. How could She use them against me?"

"I know them, and I gave you the address. Death knew you were looking for Answer so She played a trick on you. On us."

Núr peeked around my side.

"It came out the back."

That was good news. As she cleaned the wound, I kept up the story to take my mind off the pain.

"Death told me She didn't want me looking for Despair. I think She had something to do with it. She could sense in my intention that I was searching for Her, so the search for Despair must lead to Death."

Núr dried the alcohol from around the entrance wound and pressed a gauze bandage onto it.

"But why? Death would want Despair to stay missing?"

"Seriously," I winced. "You'd think the two of Them would be the best of besties."

"Or maybe the search for Despair leads to *your* death."

She didn't look up after that, just wiped the exit wound with alcohol in silence, on her knees and leaning around me.

Despite the sharp pains from my back, my mind still found the energy to take a long, intense look at the heart-shaped bulb of Núr's jeans. A thin band of smooth brown skin was visible between her belt and the bottom of the t-shirt. I felt a sudden sympathy for the men she had snared in her study of the Sisters.

She pressed another gauze square to my back.

"I cannot ask you to go on, Mr. Oliver."

She sat up straight, looking me in the eye.

"But I will pay you what you are due, so far, and drive you to an emergency room."

For a moment, I thought about the possible consequences of continuing the case, but for some reason I couldn't bring myself to give in. Was I still under Curiosity's spell, or grasping for a Get-Out-Of-Death-Free card? No way to be sure.

Maybe I was just sick of the Safe New World.

"I'm not done."

I pushed off from the white meditation mat, onto which my blood had stained a dark archipelago. It was surprising how little pain I felt as I stood up.

Núr put a hand on my elbow. I shook my head.

"Before, I was afraid to ask Curiosity how to find Answer, but I think I am just going to risk it."

"Mr. Oliver, with Misfortune and Death waiting for you, not to mention the Sisters..."

"No offense, but can you give me this lecture on the way over to my office? I need to pick up a few things."

»–«

Hardboiled is the proper attitude in which to wrangle with angels.

Núr had attempted to eat, pray, and love her way through it, and look where that got her: a lot of broken hearts in her wake and a final, desperate email to a detective agency. She had to jump genre.

What does this bum mean by *hardboiled*, you ask? I think it's pretty simple. Hardboiled, noir, call it what you will, is a story in which the Hero and the Rough are the same fellow. Or, the same dame, as the case might be.

And what exactly is a Rough?

Call him morally conflicted, semi-civilized, liminal, anti-hero, whatever you like. Rough is really the best way to describe him. He gets knocked around, manipulated, shot, knifed, lied to, and slammed against the street in the pouring rain, yet he just keeps coming back for more until the story is done.

I don't normally think of myself in this role—I *normally* try to keep things safe and simple—but, sitting in the passenger seat of Núr's little hybrid with stripes on my back and holes in my hands, feet, and gut, well ... Denying the archetypes doesn't make them go away, now does it?

The Rough has always been there, hanging out with the Hero, ever since Prince Gilgamesh fell in love with wild hairy Enkidu back in Sumerian times. Maybe the Hero and Rough are not always *that* close, but Ennis del Mar played a pretty good Rough to Jack Twist in that little flip-flop where it was Enkidu who ended up mourning Gilgamesh instead of the other way around.

And, don't shake your head. Did you know that the name Enkidu means "from Enki" who was (among other things) the Sumerian *dios del mar*? Mm-hmm. Still think I broke the back of that analogy?

As Núr drove down Fig Lane, the toothy hills of the cemetery strobed in flashes of the storm, and my mood was drawn down to the hundreds entombed there whose conversations with Death had not ended quite so well as mine. Watching the gravestones scroll past the window beyond Núr's intense, wet-street-driving stare, I wondered who had been the first buried there, and what his appointment with Death had been like.

And, this was just one of the city's many cemeteries. In fact, I suddenly realized, the dead were the greatest population dynamic. In my city, in any city. In the entire world was Death's trash can.

I felt the wheel in my hands. Why was I driving? I looked to my right.

Death was sitting there, black lips smirking. One snowy hand reached over to my thigh.

"Road head?"

I pulled my right hand from the wheel and jabbed the thumb into the bullet wound.

"What happened?" Núr said. "Are you okay?"

I held both hands on my side. Fuck, that hurt.

"I made a mistake. I slipped into the other world for a second."

"How? What did you see?"

"Nothing. Just enough to know I had broken my mind thinking stupid, dark thoughts."

She sighed.

"You must tame that dark side of yourself, Mr. Oliver."

Yeah.

Like it or not, I had become the Rough in my own story. I had leapt into the Abyss, made my home in the Wilderness, stepped across the tracks into the Wrong Side of town. I was, as the Sage put it, living in a van down by the river.

It was an old, old role.

Robin Hood had his Little John. Even Jesus had his wild, hair-wearing cousin Juan Bautista who—just like when Little John confronted Robin on that bridge—greeted the Hero mid-stream.

The genius of the hardboiled is to drag the whole story into the roiling water by making the Rough the same guy as the Hero. Ever notice how it's raining all the time in noir flicks and detective stories? The City of Angels has never seen as much rain is it does in *The Big Sleep*; water, water, everywhere and a dark, ravenous sump at the end for your trouble.

Why the hell do you think that is? Because the hardboiled Rough is in the middle of the Jordan the whole time, holding his own head under water.

Turning onto Pine Street, Núr slid a little on the slick pavement, and whispered what I guess was an apology in Arabic. Not wanting her to feel bad about it, I laughed it off.

"Straightened it out like a pro."

She gave me a brief, sideways, gorgeous smile.

So yeah, Núr is on my side in this little adventure, but do I take her as my Heroine? No, no, she's a client, pure and simple. A dangerous, beautiful, mysterious client, but still just a client. The hardboiled Rough doesn't need a Hero getting in the way, with all that Heroic naïveté and silly ideas.

It's not for nothing that cuckolded Miles Archer gets iced in the hollow between chapters one and two, leaving the satan-faced Sam Spade on his own. And, the best thing about casting Harrison Ford in *Blade Runner*? We got to watch Han Solo on his own—as the name itself implies—without that angsty kid Skywalker mucking things up with his "hokey religion" and daddy issues.

When Solo stood face-to-face with Ira's dark little puppet in Cloud City, he drew his gun like a good Rough should. And, if I had been playing the good Rough, I never would have let Núr talk me out of taking my pistol on this case. But, I was on my way to remedy that little mistake.

Even if a clip full of hot lead couldn't permanently dispatch one of the Messengers, it could get Her out of my hair for a while.

Of course, in Hollywood's sugar-sweet vision, Solo gets frozen and Little Orphan Jedi saves him in the next episode, then goes on to win over daddy's heart. But, in the real world, do you think Darth Ira is going to go all weepy and toss Empress Vana into the Abyss because the Hero is getting the lunch shocked out of him?

Of course not. The angel of Rage has sent trillions of sentient beings to their deaths—watching American Graffiti bite it with blue sparks flying out of his teeth is not going to move Her, even if he is Her little boy.

A blaster shot to the breastplate might have gotten Her attention, though.

And it's not for nothing that Frodo Baggins, despite his Heroic Ring-bearing escapades, never stared Sauron in the face except by accident. Oh no, it was the scruffy *ranger* who picked up that Skype-enabled crystal ball and punk-dialed the Devil.

And, Will Turner's blood might have saved the day at the end of that first *Pirates of the Caribbean* movie. But, who dived into death to make that possible? The Rough, Jack Sparrow.

My point? You've got to be Rough to dance with angels, my friend.

»-«

As Núr pulled up outside C. R. Oliver Investigations, I realized she had spared me the lecture and left me to my thoughts. After the quiet drive over, she parked, cranked off the key, and took a deep breath.

"Why are you doing this? Surely my fee is not enough for you to risk your life."

How could I tell Núr that her fee was no longer my primary motivator? Then again, how could I tell myself that I was squaring off against Death and all the hostiles of the other world in order to find a way to avoid Death and all of the hostiles of the other world?

I was swinging on paradoxes, but how better to finally get the hang of how angels work? We stepped out of the car and considered each other over the roof of it.

I shrugged.

"Can you despair of finding Despair? The moment you're convinced you'll never find Her, there She is."

I stepped around the car and limped for the office door. Núr followed, pressed her key fob. The little hybrid beeped twice like a bike horn.

"And then, hope renewed, you lose Her again."

I fumbled the key with my cut hands like a monkey at a peg board, finally forced the damn thing into the lock, and got us inside.

"It is confusing, I confess," she said as I stepped over to the file cabinet. "It is like dancing with a shadow."

I shuffled through the junk in the top file drawer until I found an old hip-flask, a joke present from my cousin Chuchi when I opened the detective agency.

"Mr. Oliver," Núr started.

"There's some bourbon in the back of the refrigerator."

I nodded for her to get it. She cocked her head.

"To manage inhibitions," I said. "If necessary and in moderation."

She was still neither moved nor moving, so I stepped past her and opened the fridge. There were tall twin bottles of bourbon behind the water and power drinks: a nearly empty Temptation green-label straight and a brand new, red-label Redemption high rye. I grabbed the full bottle.

"Abstinence is also a fetish, you know."

I stripped the safety plastic from around the cap.

"Don't let your virtues turn into vices."

"Do not imagine that your vices are virtues."

I ignored her, carefully poured a thin stream of booze into the flask.

"Mr. Oliver," she started again.

"Aren't we past the formalities, sweetheart?"

I capped off the flask, stuffed it into my back pocket.

"Call me Charles."

"Charles, you are fired."

I grabbed my duster from the coat rack. As I slipped my arms into it, I could see she had a serious look on her face. Almost a pout.

"Looks like you found Her. Case closed."

She chuckled, in spite of herself. From night to day in zero point five seconds.

"Or, maybe not."

I stepped over to the desk.

"Even so, this approach has become too dangerous."

"This approach has gotten dangerous because I've gotten close."

I slid open the drawer, grabbed the pistol, checked the clip.

"Mr. Oliver, I told you: when facing angels, you cannot put your faith in a firearm."

I shrugged and stuffed the pistol into the back of my trousers.

"This is probably not going to end well anyway."

ON THE HEAD OF A PIN

PART SIX

A light rain fell on Pressure as I stepped up to the entrance. The rolling bass of swing jazz made the neon olives vibrate. I had considered going through the back again, but decided that I was done sneaking around.

"You are a persistent little shit, aren't you?"

Misfortune kicked off the wall and began long-striding across the pavement to intercept me.

"Well, I *am* prone to setbacks."

I drew the pistol from behind me and leveled it at Her face.

"But aren't we all?"

She stopped in place, but was still grinning.

"Sending me home to Mama? That won't keep me away forever, Chucky."

I shrugged and drew the hammer back until it clicked.

"I don't need forever, Missy."

"But have you thought about this—"

She cocked an eyebrow.

"What if it *misfires*?"

"Then I get an opportunity to do what I really want, which is wring Your little green neck with my bare hands."

She bit Her bottom lip.

"You're a fun one, Chuck."

She executed a sarcastically deep stage bow, one arm waving me toward the door.

As I circled around Her with the gun still aimed solidly at Her *jasad*, She giggled.

"Like I said before, it's your funeral."

»-«

Inside, the lights were a steadily incandescent red, white, and blue over a swirling galaxy of zoot suits and knee-length flapper skirts. Angels and dross spun in little orbits, locked hands substituting for gravity. A frenzied, big-band version of *Cheek to Cheek* was roaring from the sound system, but there were no cheeks touching in this crowd.

I scanned the floor. Invidia was out there in Her silver minidress, cutting in on one couple after another, but Curiosity was nowhere to be seen.

I maneuvered around the dance floor, edged along the bar. Avarice locked fierce eyes on me as I passed, lemon yellow bra heaving.

"Is that a hip flask?! No outside drinks!"

It figures that She could detect a lost profit even through a long coat and pants pocket. I pulled my wallet from the other hip and flipped it to Her, Frisbee-style. She blinked and caught it in both hands.

"Charge me for a whole bottle of bourbon. Top shelf, if You want."

Socordia turned from where She was still pretending to wash Her hands, and gave me a curious look. I kept moving, angling past the DJ table where Luxury and Ira stood side by side, in turns glaring at me and whispering in each other's ears.

Vana was leaning against the wall once again: gold dress, black fedora tipped forward on Her head, drawing deep on a long cigarette. She scanned me top to toe as I walked toward the rear exit, blew a fountain of smoke into the air between us.

"You're better dressed than last time," She said flatly.

By the back door, Gula stood as dark and earthy as Her daughter was light and airy. For a moment She said nothing, measuring me up, then nodded.

"She's upstairs."

I nodded back and turned toward the door. But, then, I thought maybe She was being intentionally vague. Did She mean Curiosity, Answer, or Despair?

I needed more.

"You need more," She grinned. "To be properly fortified."

She was seeing me. I wasn't used to that. Núr didn't get me. Her little stool-frog hostess didn't get me. The gay kids in the alley hadn't gotten me. Curiosity hadn't gotten me. Gula's Sisters hadn't gotten me.

I rubbed the stamp on my hand. Why not be honest?

"I need Your Kid to get me to Answer. And, I need Answer for personal reasons, but also to get me to Despair."

"Those last two could be the same."

Her dark brown eyes were like the weight of the Earth on my chest. I felt like She was charging me like an elephant, or like a mammoth, some ancient Intelligence challenging my primitive, caveman hubris with Her raw power.

But, without malice. A challenge to challenge me to be better.

"My personal reasons," the PIN. in my private thoughts, "might lead me to Despair?"

She rolled Her eyes playfully.

"She was our Sister, once. Before She ruined the party. She was the first of Us to see and recognize Death. To see that We lead souls to Her."

"The wages of the Sins," I said.

She nodded with an ample grin. She inhaled, Her breasts pressing against cloth. For a moment, I considered a romp with Curiosity's Mother, but stifled it.

She grinned at me conspiratorially.

"Curiosity is upstairs. Maybe She'll lead you to Answer, which might help you find Despair."

"Maybe?"

She leaned in and put a hand on my elbow.

"My Daughter is good with questions. Not so good with answers."

»–«

"I didn't think you were coming back!"

"I wasn't going to. My client scolded me for cavorting with the Fallen."

Curiosity giggled, leaning on the door and rubbing Her left calf with Her right foot.

"We're not fallen, silly. You are."

"Me?"

"You singular, you plural. What a crummy language you have."

She shook Her head with a smirk.

"*We* exist in superposition, innocent and fallen at once. You determine which face you see."

She stepped forward, slipped an arm over my shoulder.

"If you make Us snakes, We spew poison. If you make Us friends,
 We help you out."

"Well, then I guess You're innocent to me."

I put a hand on Her waist.

"You haven't gotten me to do anything I wouldn't normally do."

"Did you come back for a replay?"

"No."

Better soften it up a bit, Chuck.

"Well, not yet. I came to see if You knew where I might find an
 angel called Answer."

"She lives in number seven—"

"Yeah, I know, in the penthouse." I nodded toward the floor. "But,
 I'm not eager to head back down there. Does She ever come up, get
 around, maybe hang out in the club?"

Curiosity looked at me sideways with that grin I mistook for
 Mischief when I first saw Her.

"Aren't you a detective, Chuck?"

"Yeah, why?"

"Wouldn't a detective *normally* go check out the scene of the
 crime?" She slipped an arm over my shoulder.

"What crime? Are You saying Despair was kidnapped or—" I wasn't sure if an angel could be said to be murdered.

"No, no ... but whatever happened, wouldn't you," She slipped the other arm over my other shoulder, "*normally* go to the missing Person's residence and take a look around?"

Stump me, She was right. Why the hell hadn't I thought of that?

"You mean Despair's old place?"

She grinned with those lips I longed to see wrapped again around my manhood.

"Her place is just down the hall."

I gathered myself. Might be safer heading to Despair's former digs than back downstairs in search of Answer.

Before I could think too hard on it, Curiosity smiled, grabbed my hand, and pulled me down the hallway.

"Come on, let's dance."

»–«

As you might expect, Despair's apartment was in grayscale. In the foyer mirror, even blonde, blushing, blue-eyed Curiosity's reflection was about as colorful as a charcoal drawing. I scanned the place for just a hint of simple white or black.

Nothing but gray.

Bookcases and cabinets were crowded into every corner, coated in dust, packed with oddities and artifacts in various states of disarray and decay. Faded photographs were everywhere, scattered under desks, stacked on shelves, piled like snowdrifts in the corners.

"There's *so* much cool stuff here," Curiosity cooed.

A stray hair clung to the back of a chaise longue. I pinched it and held it out.

"What color was Your Aunt's hair?"

"Gray, of course." She waggled Her head. Not sure what that waggle meant, but the hair I was holding up was gray. Like everything else in the place.

"Show me one of Yours."

Curiosity turned, grinned, twirled a spiral of blonde on one finger.

I wanted to sigh, but I swallowed it and forced a chuckle. I realized She was indulging Herself in me.

"I mean, pluck it."

She pinched a single strand with both hands, pulled it free, and gave it to me. I held the two hairs out in a tattered table lamp's drab effort at light.

Curiosity's dead hair was tightly curled, but now simply a lighter, tin-like gray compared to the wavy, dark gray hair I had found on the chair.

"Not what you expected?"

She eased over toward a china cabinet filled with a variety of mugs, cups, and glasses. No doubt, each had been employed by someone in a final act of self-poisoning.

I shrugged.

"I half expected the walls to be covered in Van Goghs."

She spun around, smile wide, and bounced on the balls of Her feet.

"Even better!"

She nodded toward the mantel. Centered, in a glass case, was an antique revolver. In case you didn't know, Van Gogh murdered himself with a revolver to the chest.

"Jesus. Is that ..."

"The very one."

She pointed at Her left breast, made a "pssh" sound, and closed Her eyes with Her tongue flopping out one side of Her mouth.

"Your Aunt," I said, "is seriously into Her sin."

"Well, you know ... when you call Her My *Aunt* ..."

Curiosity squinted at me, as if to gauge my readiness for what She was about to say.

"She's not really like the other Sisters."

"What do You mean?"

I flipped over an envelope, couldn't read the weird writing on the front.

Curiosity picked up a letter opener from a coffee table, spun it between Her fingers.

"Vana came out first, shining like a spotlight. Then the Twins, Luxury and Ira, came out together."

She locked eyes with me, still spinning the desk blade in Her fingers.

"Lýpe was the shadow that the two of Them cast from Vana's light."

"They 'came out'? Came out *from where?*"

Curiosity bit the corner of Her lip to keep from smiling and set the letter opener carefully on the mantel beside Van Gogh's pistol. Apparently, I had asked the magic question.

"Do you want Me to show you?"

I was immediately struck with an intense desire for Her not to show me. In fact, I nearly backed up at the thought of it, gripped with an inexplicable anxiety.

Then, I heard a whimpering.

Curiosity scanned the room like one of Spielberg's velociraptors, glanced at both doorways. The whimpering grew into sobbing. I looked around, but couldn't see anyone. Or Anyone.

"Meow?" Curiosity taunted. "Little fraidy cat, where are You?"

"Who—" I started.

There was a disturbance in the corner of the room. A pale blue foot withdrew into a mound of quilts. Curiosity saw it too, leaped over to the pile, and started flinging aside the covers one by one.

"Who is that?" I asked. The hidden angel screamed like a stuck animal from under the last few quilts.

Curiosity turned to me and rolled Her eyes.

"Fear."

"What the hell is She doing here?"

The last cover was thrown aside, revealing a shivering, whimpering figure in the fetal position, barefoot in a tattered white dress, skin pale and a wild mane of hair as blue as deep water.

"She's Lýpe's kid."

Curiosity shook Her head in disdain.

"She's been here, lame and useless, ever since Her Mother disappeared."

Fear turned, eyes like rings of turquoise flashed at me.

"Why is *he* here?"

"Heeee's looking for Your Maaama," Curiosity sing-songed.

"Maybe She's trapped in a dark, dark place. Or maybe She was taken by the Ad-ver-sar-eeeeee."

Fear cried out at every stressed syllable.

"Cut it out," I said.

"Oh, She's not going to help you, Chuck. Even if She was here when whatever happened happened, She would have covered Her eyes and ears the whole time."

Curiosity leaned over Fear's trembling body and started poking Her in the ribs.

"*Even* if *Someone* was *ripping* Her *Mother* to *little pieces*!"

ON THE HEAD OF A PIN

Fear let out a wail, and I felt like someone was stuffing every wound in my battered body with the business end of a cigar. I grabbed Curiosity by the arm and pulled Her back.

"I said cut it out!"

Fear took that opportunity to scramble across the floor, away from Curiosity. She lifted Herself to Her feet on the chaise longue, nearly colliding with Her grayed-out reflection in the foyer mirror as She fled out the door.

"Run, run, You little orphaned brat!" Curiosity shouted.

I let go of Her arm with a shove.

"What the hell is wrong with You?"

She sneered.

"You *would* sympathize with Her. You both only want to know two things: where Her Mother is and how to beat Death."

This Chick had wasted enough of my time. I was done with Her. I rushed out the door after Fear, looking both ways in the corridor.

She was gone.

I noticed the hairs were still pinched between thumb and finger in my left hand. Outside of Lýpe's colorless apartment, Curiosity's plucked curl was once again golden blonde, but the hair I found on the chaise longue was now as black as a midnight sea.

»–«

When I got downstairs to the club, Fear was pleading with Her Aunts, weeping and hysterical, tugging their wrists and clothes.

The swing jazz was still booming from the speakers but several couples had stopped dancing to watch the spectacle.

"Please, Lux, I can't take it! I'm terrified something awful—"

"You're always terrified, Gorgeous," Luxury purred, stroking Her niece's cheek. Fear pulled away and turned to Ira.

"Aren't You mad that—"

Ira jerked Her blazer out of Fear's grip.

"I'm mad that You're ruining Our party!"

"You're bad for business, Kid!" Avarice shouted from the bar.

Gula saw me standing by the door, grabbed Fear's hand and led Her to me. This was going to be bad.

"Who got Her all worked up? Was it you?"

She jabbed a cinnamon fingernail in my face, then pointed beside me.

"Or was it You?"

I turned and there was Curiosity, smirking like a bird-stuffed cat. Gula shook Her head, grabbed Curiosity's arm.

"All three of You, come over here."

Gula dragged the two younger angels by Their wrists to the corner where the long spaces behind the bar and DJ table met. Fear kept casting nervous glances at me over Her shoulder. Curiosity finally noticed and gave Her cousin a cruel shove with Her free hand.

Gula let go of Them and spun with a fierce Angry Mother face, but then gasped, horn pendant dancing in alarm. We all turned to see what She was looking at.

Misfortune was standing at the other end of the DJ booth, scanning the dance floor.

One by one, Gula grabbed our shoulders and shoved us down behind the bar—first Fear, then me, then Curiosity—and She didn't have to shove hard. It was clear, to me at least, what Misfortune stepping into the club from the rear meant.

She had been downstairs to tattle to Her Mother.

We crawled the length of the bar, maneuvering around Socordia's and Avarice's legs. I noticed my wallet on the counter beside the register, so I reached up and snatched it as I scooted by.

Once we were at the end, Fear curled Herself into a whimpering ball, but Curiosity and I edged up to the end of the bar, got to our knees, and peered over the top.

Ira was shouting at Misfortune, but I couldn't hear what She was yelling over the music. As stiff as a general, She pointed to the front door, but the little green witch just stared back impassively.

 Holding out an upturned fist as Ira continued to fume, Misfortune slowly unrolled Her middle finger, turned it downward, and lowered it to the DJ table.

In a spray of sparks and a flicker of the overhead lights, the music stopped.

The crowd on the dance floor stumbled to a halt and turned to the Sisters for an explanation. There were shouts and groans and mumbling, all of which fell quiet when Ira backhanded Misfortune hard enough to send Her spinning to the floor.

Then, there was a long, long silence.

Socordia turned from the sink to see what was going on, and Avarice slowly closed the register drawer. Invidia put Her hand to Her own cheek, mouth wide open. Vana stubbed out Her cigarette and took off the fedora. Gula and Luxury simply shook Their heads in disbelief while Ira stepped back from Misfortune, chest still heaving but the fury of the moment drained away.

"Awesome," came Curiosity's voice from over my shoulder.

But then, it felt like someone had kicked open a door during a winter storm. I heard Fear gasp behind us, and started to turn, but Curiosity grabbed my arm.

"No, look, look!"

Tendrils of dark mist crept around the edges of the back door of the club at all angles, like the tentacles of a huge octopus, tracing their way along the inside walls. Misfortune's fallen body was coiled in smoke and dragged back into the shadows as limp as a pillowcase full of pool balls. As She disappeared, a billowing thunderhead lifted through the darkness like a great inky skull of cloud.

Death stepped through the storm, black minidress caressing Her thighs as She strutted into the room, muscles rippling under ice-white skin. She planted black stilettos wide and took a long, deep breath.

"I told You," She spoke into the audial void, "just to enjoy Your damned parties and stop indulging that nosy hunk of meat who barged into My home."

A green-suited dross on the dance floor stepped forward.

ON THE HEAD OF A PIN

"Who *is* this bitch?"

Several others, angels among them, laughed.

Death's frown slowly widened into a grin.

"Let me demonstrate."

There was a metallic pop from overhead. Before he could look up, the guy in the green suit was crushed against the dance floor by a light fixture the size of a bar stool.

The crowd erupted into a bonfire of curses and threats: "What the fuck?!" and "Get out of here!" and "Turn the music back on!"

Not only did they seem to have no fear, but no sense of consequence whatsoever. Through the swirling blaze of fists waving at Death, I could see Her smile widen.

Near the far wall, a flapper in a cloche hat slipped on a spilled drink, her head smacking hard against the edge of a table on the way down. She slumped over a chair and slid limply to the floor.

"I have to put a stop to this," I said.

"Ooh, what are you going to do?" Curiosity beamed.

Fear reached out, put Her hand on my ankle, and looked up.

"Be careful."

"This is the safest thing for everyone, Sugar, given the circumstances."

I stood up and strode purposefully across the club. I had to shoulder my way through the idiots on the dance floor, who were still not getting the message that Death was staring them in the face. Death, however, did not fail to notice me.

"Charles!"

She held Her arms out in a mock embrace.

"I did not know you were here, which means you are still being a *very* ..."

A goateed guy just ahead of me clutched his left arm and crumpled to the floor.

"... *bad* ..."

A girl in a red skirt leaned against the DJ table and, with a crackle of sparks, jerked and fell on her side.

"... *boy*!"

A pencil-thin punk to my left tripped over his own zipper boots and tumbled to the floor, the bottle in his hand ending up stuffed into his eye socket.

I reached under the duster, around my back, and felt the warm grip of the pistol. What the hell are you doing, Chuck old boy? Can you deal Death to Herself?

Only one way to find out. I drew the pistol as I cleared the crowd, and leveled it at Her snowy cleavage. The room was suddenly silent again, and we stood there for a beat, contemplating one Another.

"Sending Me to My room without supper?"

"I'll bring You down a snack later."

ON THE HEAD OF A PIN

She tilted Her head back, knowingly.

"I knew you could not resist that kiss for long."

"See You soon," I said, and unloaded into Her.

ACT III

PART SEVEN

Even after the *jasad* of Death imploded in a whirling braid of cold light and black smoke, the party-goers at Pressure simmered, muttering and heckling the Sisters, as if several of them were not scattered about the dance floor in various states of post-mortem disarray.

The Sisters whipped concerned faces back and forth like the coaching staff of a losing baseball team. Finally, Vana stepped into the space recently vacated by Death.

"Closing time! Everyone out!"

"Pssshh," a man in a trilby hat waved dismissively. "Just clean this shit up and let's get back to the party."

Was this guy serious? I turned and leveled the pistol at the hat, or just below it.

"You heard the Lady."

The clip was empty, but he didn't know that. Even so, he just laughed.

"Whaya gonna do? Shoot me? The angels here can fix me right up."

"Can..." started Luxury, behind me.

Ira finished: "...but won't."

The trilby hat guy rolled his eyes and put his palms out.

"Whatever, alright."

He, and everyone else, began shuffling toward the door, grumbling. I pocketed the pistol and started to follow them out. A hand took mine from behind, skin so warm it could only be an angel's, so I stopped and turned.

"You," Vana flipped my hand over to show me the stamp, half-hidden by Núr's bandage, "can stay."

»-«

After the floor emptied, the lights went up white and bright, revealing a chaos of crushed plastic cups, spilled drinks, cigarette butts, bits of half-eaten food, used condoms, hypodermic needles, dead bodies, and a crumpled light fixture.

Invidia shoved a mop into Curiosity's hand.

"Don't You want to know how it feels to clean up a mess You helped make?"

"Me?" She put the fingertips of Her free hand against Her chest.

"You know how I know."

Invidia fondled a silver pendant dangling in Her cleavage. It looked like a set of scales.

Curiosity shrugged and took the mop in both hands.

"I bet there's some cool stuff out there."

"Oliver." Gula nodded at the guy in the green suit under the crumpled light. "Can you drag them out to the sidewalk? The Girls and I need to have a talk."

"To the sidewalk," I confirmed.

"Don't worry. Someone will be around shortly to pick them up."

I could tell from Her inflection that "someone" was Someone, so I just did as I was asked.

As I dropped the last corpse on the curb and yanked the bottle from his eye, an antique, black van turned the corner with glaring bright headlights. Right on cue.

I tossed the bloodied bottle in a trash can. The van shuddered to a halt, but the lights stayed on. The driver door opened with a creak and an old man in a black suit stepped out, glaring at me with fierce, blue-gray eyes.

He ground his teeth and slammed the door behind him.

"You were expecting a skeleton in a robe with a scythe?"

I was. I was also wondering Who He was and why He was not Death Herself.

He grinned and bent to grab the wrist of the electrocuted girl.

"Death is the Predator. I am the Scavenger."

He dragged her to the back of the van with surprisingly little difficulty. With His free hand, He lifted the rear door and flung the body inside like a bag of garbage.

"Should I help?"

He grinned as He shuffled toward the second corpse.

"You can't," He chuckled. "Not now that I am here."

I tried to nudge the goateed guy with my monk-strap. He was as stiff and solid as stone.

"You work with Her, then?"

He flung the second body into the van and rolled His eyes.

"I am Her garbage man."

He shook his head, gray curls swaying around His ears.

"She has always been lazy. She's never had to work for Her dinner. The whole of Creation funnels souls Her way. But, lately? Even more."

Is that so? My detective brain kicked in. How lately was "lately"? Since I had showed up? Since Despair went missing?

"More lazy lately?"

He stopped, grinned, and wagged his bony finger at me.

"Just because I clean up Her messes doesn't mean I'm going to clean up yours."

Fair enough. I needed to answer those questions with my own brain cells.

"But," he grumbled, "Death used to take care of the clubbers Herself, instead of leaving them to … mere Misfortune."

I chuckled.

"You might be surprised to know She killed all of these Herself."

He cocked His head at me.

"Did She now?"

I nodded, gave Him a two-fingered salute, and turned to head back into the club. But then, I had a thought.

"Why are You a man?"

He tossed a corpse into the van and grinned at me.

"All of the other angels are female."

He waved me off as He shuffled toward the last corpse.

"They're responses to your consciousness. But, I suspect, you understand that already. You made your way here, after all."

That wasn't really an answer. I took a short breath, lifted a finger, and stepped forward.

Those sharp, blue-gray eyes flashed at me like a threat.

"When you and I meet next, Charles Roland Oliver, you won't really be there anymore."

»-«

I stepped back inside Pressure to head downstairs and finish the case. The Sisters were still seated at the bar, like They had been the whole time Curiosity and I were cleaning up, but their powwow was clearly over. They all turned to look at me.

"You came here looking for Lýpe," Ira stated with a tone of absolute certainty. The top button of Her strict burgundy suit jacket was undone, and my brain raced trying to figure out what that little aberration might mean.

"Come here. We need to talk."

"It's okay," said Luxury, brushing a red curl from Her face. "We may be able to help each other."

Gula was standing behind the bar, tall and strong like a bronze statue, Her arm over the shoulder of Fear, who was shivering and nursing a cup of tea. Avarice was beside Them, an orange jacket providing a bit more coverage than She had a few minutes ago. As I took a seat at the bar, She slid a mug in front of me.

"Coffee or tea?"

I must have hesitated, because She added, "On the house."

This was intriguing.

"Coffee. Black."

"I think maybe I should fill him in," said Invidia as I took my first sip. I should not have been surprised at how smooth the coffee tasted, considering that it was brewed by angels, but I was.

"Curiosity had something to do with Lýpe's disappearance."

She fondled Her pendant.

"I can sense it."

I turned to look over each shoulder.

"Curiosity, what happened to Despair?"

But She was gone, run off to explore some new fancy, no doubt.

"Don't bother," Socordia said. "Curiosity couldn't give you a straight answer even if She tried."

"And," Luxury said, "Despair is not a good name for Her."

She tilted Her head and turned to Her Sisters for confirmation.

"Regret?"

"*Awareness of Consequences*," Ira stated definitively. "She only becomes Despair when mortals try to take the long view and they can't let go of ... things."

Socordia put Her hand over mine.

"If Death is up to something, We would have you tell Us what you know."

Aha, so we had come to the scene where the detective lays out his evidence. And, since I wasn't living a cozy whodunit, the crook was already identified and not among those actually in the room.

"Here's what I know." I counted them in my head. "Three things. One, Misfortune and Death both got in my way when I tried to visit Answer."

"Answer?" Socordia laughed once. "Don't bother with Her, either. None of Us have ever seen Her."

"Or We're all seeing Her all the time," Invidia added, mysteriously.

"Two," I continued, to get back on track. "Death told me that She could sense I was looking for Despair. Or, Awareness."

"—of Consequences," Ira completed it.

"Yeah, so. That means the search for Lýpe leads to Death, yeah?"

I looked around at Them for confirmation.

Ira nodded.

"Everything eventually does, but this is obviously more direct."

I shrugged.

"Third, I found one of Death's hairs in Despair's apartment."

Fear let out a sob. Gula squeezed Her Niece's shoulder and slowly shook Her head.

"That One was created with a hunger that will never be satisfied."

"She'd take Us all if She could," said Avarice, refilling my mug.

"Oh Ava," Ira said, "She can and She will. One day."

Vana closed Her eyes. "The universe conspires to give Her everything She wants. Life is a struggle against Her. It's the most fundamental alchemy of Creation."

Invidia let out a puff of air, and fondled Her necklace.

"Not today. Death is unduly interested in you, Mr. Oliver. I believe that somehow you can set this right."

"The only thing I haven't figured out is Her angle. What did She do with Despair and why?"

"Charles," Avarice leaned on Her elbows toward me. "Isn't it more important that you undo whatever it is Death has done with Her, even if you don't get to know *why* She did it?"

Good point. I had indulged Curiosity too much already.

The Sisters seemed transformed by their encounter with Death. Mama Gula was showing fortitude I had not seen when She was scoffing at Her Daughter's dalliance. Avarice was more prudent than greedy, Socordia more restrained than lazy. And Invidia was simply eager for justice.

"One thing is certain," Ira cautioned, taking a deep breath that strained the blood-red buttons on Her suit jacket. "Death will not be easily foiled."

"But," Luxury countered, "there's always a chance."

Vana leaned over, sliding a few things across the bar: the black fedora, a packet of cigarettes with a white gazelle logo, and a red lighter etched with what looked like a row of green stripes and ribbons. With eyes full of fear, She nodded for me to take them. I scooped up the lighter and flipped the cap open.

What the hell was I getting myself into? The eldest of the Seven was running scared, yet I was unable to locate a shred of hesitation. Had I lost my mind? Or found it?

I caught myself staring at the pendant resting in Invidia's cleavage, the silver scales made up of a perfect cross, two perfect triangles, and two perfect semi-circles.

Ira set the hat on my head and leveled it off. "Why did you go down there in the first place?"

"Just to ask where Lýpe went?" Luxury tapped out a smoke and set it on my lip.

I thumbed the lighter and took a puff. Might as well come out with it.

"I wanted to know my PIN."

They cast amused glances at each other, then started laughing all at once. Even Fear chuckled a little.

Ira put a hand on my shoulder.

"Charles, this whole case is your PIN. You've been dancing on it from the beginning. You cast Our roles yourself, even if We've been doing the acting. Knowing your PIN is as simple as looking around to orient yourself to your own perceptions."

"Not that it's such an easy thing for your kind to do," Invidia said, "but you're getting better at it."

Avarice refilled Fear's cup with tea.

"You're also a synecdoche of your culture's PIN, which is why Miss Lucas is concerned that some sort of Apocalypse is in the works."

"Cynic duck what? Try that again in English."

I checked the magazine of the pistol in a hope against hope that there was at least one slug left. There wasn't.

"You're like a spider on a cultural web," Socordia said. "You feel its vibrations."

Gula leaned in.

"Or, like tofu. You take on its flavor."

"Great. I'm the cosmic tofu?"

I waggled the empty magazine at Them, hoping They might have something more useful to offer than goofy parables. Avarice shook Her head at my implied question, then went straight back to the metaphors:

"Or the other way, like a bay leaf in soup, you can infuse it with flavor."

"Or like a tent post," Invidia said, "you can lift the whole tent."

"I think I got the idea."

I slid the useless pistol down the bar. The effort tugged at the bullet wound in my gut, as if to remind me Whose place I was about to revisit.

"Your girlfriend Núr isn't being as helpful as she could be," Luxury said, moving around the bar to the stool where I was sitting. She swept red curls bchind Her ears, stopped between my knees, and started unbuttoning my shirt. I slid back against the bar.

"Calm down, sweetie." She grinned with Her tongue in the corner of Her mouth. "I'm in new form tonight. I just want to see where you painted your clothes, and look! It's all gone."

She held the shirt open for me to see. The gunshot wound was healed and Núr's bandage gone. I had to sweep the skin with my own hand to believe it. That's when I noticed that the wraps on my hands were gone too, and there was no sign of the gashes.

When I looked up, all seven of the Sisters were gathered around my bar stool. Luxury whipped the fedora from my head and They all leaned in to kiss me at once, the incredible heat from Their lips burning a band across my forehead.

Ira took the hat from Her Sister and set it carefully back on my skull.

"Charles, there is no sense killing Death where She dwells in your PIN. She doesn't need a *jasad* there."

"I'm not going down there to kill Her. I don't have any bullets, anyway."

"Then why? Are you going there to die?"

"I'm going down there to solve this case. And, if I can, free Lýpe."

"Good man."

She didn't look entirely convinced.

There was movement near the front door. We all turned.

Núr Lucas stood there looking like a rain-soaked kitten in dripping dark jeans and green sweatshirt, red-and-silver sneakers, and hair sticking to the sides of her face. She was wielding the rain stick like a sword, waving it at the Sisters, ready to fight.

"Mr. Oliver?"

"On my way out, doll."

She looked anxiously at the Sisters, Who had stepped away from the bar to walk across the floor and greet her.

"Daughter," Vana cupped Núr's face in both hands. "You didn't need to hunt Us like wild beasts. Just spin your dance in the other direction."

Núr fought back tears.

"I did not know how to talk to You."

Vana laughed, putting Her hands on Núr's shoulders.

"Of course you do. It's simple."

Invidia leaned in and whispered in her ear: "Don't accuse others unfairly in the name of justice."

Socordia followed: "Or show your back to a struggle out of a sense of restraint."

Gula brushed Núr's hair from her face. "Don't take from the helpless in your hunger to be strong and sturdy."

Avarice added: "or gather up more than you give, out of concern for the future."

"Don't let your certitude lead you to rash violence." Ira threw a couple of mock punches at Núr, who winced but smiled.

Luxury winked and set Her hands on Núr's hips. "And don't let the possibilities of life lead you to misuse your charms."

The Sisters formed a circle around Núr the way They had so recently formed a circle around me, and Vana lifted her chin in one hand.

ON THE HEAD OF A PIN

"You have a light in you that shines out on all the world. But, that light is not *your* light, nor does it belong to anything it shines on. You know that, don't you?"

Núr nodded and wept, and the Sisters held her to their bosoms like a lost child. She was jumping genres again, but I guess she had finally worked out her mommy issues.

It was time for me to do what I came there for, so while the Ladies were having their hugfest, I slipped out the rear door.

PART EIGHT

As I stood in the back corridor of the building, puffing on Vana's cigarette, I couldn't stop wishing I'd had the sense to pack a spare magazine. What was I going to do when I confronted Death? I had no idea. Was I off-script, or was playing it by ear the way things were supposed to go?

I heard the elevator arriving and flicked the butt onto the floor. As the doors opened, I crushed the smoke out with my shoe.

"My, my."

Misfortune was in the elevator, leaning with one arm propped on the car wall.

"Such a lot of brains, and no gun."

Figures. I *would* have to fight a Girl at this point. I lifted both fists.

"Anything you got, bud, I can take it," She said with a cold stare. Then She cracked a smile, and nodded me inside.

"Hop in. I've never seen a no-gun detective, before."

"I don't have time for a detour."

"Sometimes, Chuck, the most Misfortunate thing that can happen is I just let you do what you're already doing."

She offered me a conspiratorial grin.

"This is one of those times."

I eased into the elevator car, keeping one eye on the distance separating us. As the gates closed with an iron clank, I pulled the flask from my hip.

"Mind if I have a belt?"

"It's your funeral, handsome."

I unscrewed the cap. Something about this Chick was different, something less prawnish and homely. Maybe the light outside of Pressure had made Her look sick, bad shadows or ... something. Now, She was damned cute. I kicked back a swig of bourbon.

"Your Mom is downstairs waiting on me, I suppose."

"You suppose correctly."

As we descended, down, down into the depths of the edifice, She kept looking at me like She wanted to ask something. I held out the flask, but She shook Her head, so I swallowed a second swig and pocketed it.

I took out Vana's cigarettes, lit one. Misfortune bit Her lip and nodded at the pack, so I shook one out. She leaned toward me with the cigarette in Her lips, we touched the ends, and She drew fire from mine. Her green eyes had flecks of honey.

"Charles."

She wedged the cig between two stiff fingers and blew a cloud of smoke toward the floor of the car.

"Kiss Me."

"What?"

I checked my warning buzzers, but they were dead quiet.

"The only time I can kiss someone is when they have no concern for what happens to them."

I nodded.

"When they're courting Misfortune."

She grinned Her avocado grin.

"So to speak."

"Is that lipstick?"

She shook Her head and got a serious look. I leaned in, brushed a tear from Her cheek with my thumb, and planted one on Her lips.

Misfortune, for the record, tastes like mint.

»–«

ON THE HEAD OF A PIN

When the elevator gates parted for the second time, the door ahead had a brass V screwed to it. Nice joke. To my left was IV and to my right was VI. It was at least a compelling symmetry.

I turned to say goodbye to Misfortune, but the car was empty. The iron gates closed with a hollow clank.

I walked over to apartment VI and was momentarily tempted to keep walking to Answer's place, now that I knew where it actually was. To Hell with it. At that moment, I no longer needed to ask an angel what I wanted to do.

Instead, I stopped and took a drag on the cigarette, flipped up the collar of the duster, and pulled the fedora a bit lower in front. I listened for a moment, but it was silent. What did I expect to hear, a classical aria?

Looking down at my hands, I saw that the blood of the people I dragged out of Pressure was still smudged on the meat of my fingers.

I reached for Death's doorknob but was suddenly inspired to just kick the door in. So, that is exactly what I did.

The door spun off its hinges into emptiness. I stepped forward to see Death hunched over the cloth-covered table with shadows pouring from Her shoulders in sheets of black flame. She stood and turned, stiff-arming a pistol toward me, but I was across the room in three long strides.

I got inside Her reach, wrapped one fist around the gun, and put the knuckles of the other into Her cheek. She fell to the floor with a forearm over the velvet-draped cube. Blue eyes wide, She licked milky blood from Her dark lip with a tongue as gray as ash.

"Did You learn anything from *that* kiss?"

I stuffed Her pistol into my belt behind me.

Death growled through black teeth, rose on Her elbows, and hooked Her feet around my waist like a set of pliers.

My knees hit the floor. With a squeeze of those marble-white thighs, She pulled me down, Her legs a Chicago winter around my waist. She went for the gun with both hands. I grabbed Her wrists, and Her skin felt like frozen vodka in my hands.

She thrashed like a shark, stronger than She looked, and I shook all over from the cold and the contest. The cigarette, still clamped in my teeth, went dark in a tiny wisp of fume.

Just as I was certain She was about to reach the pistol and put a quick end to me, the cloth-covered box shook beside us, but not from our flailing. Something was moving *inside* it, and I knew that something could only be one Thing.

Death took a sudden short breath. We locked eyes and were still for a Planck moment. Or an eternity.

A burst of dark smoke hit me like a bullet train, a sphere of shadow exploding from Death's heart. I slammed against the far wall and ended up on my ass just like She was.

I shook my head and made sure I still had the pistol. Then I noticed that Death's little smoke bomb had also blown the velvet cover away. It wasn't a table. It was a cage. Inside, naked except for a leather ball-gag, was an angel with skin and hair as gray as an old barn, squatting on Her knees and staring blankly at the floor in front of Her.

Death stood, brushing off that slick, black mini-dress as if there had been something on it. Pinching the neckline to readjust it, She started slowly across the room toward me.

"I was so wrong about Curiosity being your vice. But you are a detective, so it was an honest mistake."

I pushed myself to my feet against the wall and pulled the pistol. Death stopped and gave me a one-sided grin. My hand was shaking from the cold, but I aimed the barrel squarely at Her chest.

"And, She *is* hard to resist, such a sweet bit of calico."

Death licked Her lips.

"It was Curiosity Who first turned Me on to the idea of capturing Despair."

The look on my face must have said something unflattering about Gula's little Girl, because Death laughed. She eyed the pack of cigarettes next to Her foot and knelt for it.

"She cannot help it. It is who She is."

Death stood with the smokes, and tapped one into Her mouth. The end flared with a cold, blue flame.

"If you want to reform Her, you have to reform yourself."

She was keeping Her distance, but I wanted to know my options. Glancing around, I noticed the fedora had been blown onto the shelf of the liquor cabinet beside me.

"But, you *do* have a vice, Mr. Oliver. Núr chose you to hunt for My little pet over there because you are a toy of Her Daughter."

Fear? Hardly. Awareness of Consequences must have another Daughter, and God knows I'd found plenty of long-lost relatives in my line of work. A wearisome number of them. I scooped the hat up and pushed it onto my dome.

"Cynicism."

My breath was a cloud of vapor.

"Oh, Charles," She grinned a black grin. "*You* are really good at this. Of course, Cynicism is what rubbed off Lýpe when She bumped against the Likeness, so she's a special case. Just like our girlfriend Curiosity."

"I'm not particularly cynical."

My aim had dropped to Her belly, I tried to raise it, but my muscles were cramping from the cold.

"The whole world has a bleak look these days."

She laughed, and I swear I could feel my bones weakening inside my body.

"Oh, they make a good show of rational pessimism on your world, but that is itself an indulgence, another form of play. Just look how they revel with the Sisters! Such abandon."

I glanced at Death's gimp in the cage.

"No Despair, no Awareness of Consequences."

At the sound of my voice speaking Her names, Lýpe flashed silver eyes at me.

Death held the cigarette near Her lips, pinched between finger and thumb. Her cold blue gaze leaned casually into my soul.

"If you believe there will always be a way out, endless second chances, miracle medicine for the diseases you have wooed, science to purify your polluted economy and corrupted environment."

She took a long drag.

"Or perhaps you believe all the dangers are just political lies …"

Death held Her mouth open and let a cloud of cigarette smoke pour slowly over Her bottom lip. She tilted Her head to the right.

"Well, then you can frolic in denial, yes?"

She held the cigarette in front of Her face, inspecting it.

"When there is always an imagined way to escape consequence, a *false* hope, a *false* certainty, you dance and you dance and you dance—until you die."

The blue flame winked out. She let go of the butt and watched it fall to the carpet with an open-mouthed look of faux horror.

In that moment of mockery, Her lips were gorgeously full.

I steadied the gun with my left hand and stepped away from the wall. She winked, tucked fingers into either side of Her neckline, and tugged it down to expose the tops of Her breasts, daring me to pull the trigger.

"By refusing to believe their 'glass half-full' will ever run dry, they drink like the glass is bottomless, like their vices are without cost. But, the consequences pile up before them, a colossal standing wave of destructive effects. And soon, Charlie, that wave will crash over them like The Deluge come again, and your world will be Mine."

I shivered, steadied myself against the liquor cabinet. I guess Núr's Apocalyptic conspiracy theory had turned out true.

Then it occurred to me that the Villain was revealing Her wicked plan to me in the moment of final confrontation, a trite convention that I found obnoxious. For Death's confession to make sense to my skeptical soul, this conversation had to have an ulterior motive, just like that suspicious glass of bourbon during my last visit.

But, I couldn't figure out Her scam, so I stalled.

"Suicide rates are sky high. How do You explain that?"

Death shrugged.

"She's on a leash. Sometimes I lead Her out of the cage for exercise."

Then She giggled, biting Her bottom lip.

"And, Charlie, a cynical boy like you cannot believe that everyone who rejects your sorry world is lost in Despair. After all, why are *you* here?"

Letting go of Her neckline, She started walking toward me again, shadowy wings pouring out like storm clouds behind Her. I backed up against the wall and held the pistol aimed at Her chest. There was no way out of this.

The light withdrew from Death's form like a salted snail and She was again all shadow but the cold blue disks of Her eyes. Why *was* I there? What was a mortal like me supposed to do? Ira said that Death would even take all of *Them* one day.

But, She had not yet taken Despair.

I snuck a glance. The captive angel's weary gaze was fixed on me. Death wasn't taking Despair, She was imprisoning Her, holding Her in place.

ON THE HEAD OF A PIN

In *Death's* place.

I shifted my aim and started pumping slugs into the cage. Death roared, a raging tornado of darkness with black claws spinning in all directions, shredding my clothes and my skin where they touched me, but I squeezed and squeezed and damn the consequences.

Despair jerked in Her cage at the first shot. She shuddered and spun and thrashed. And was still.

Death collapsed into Her chalky *jasad* and spun toward Her captive, lips hanging open in shock. The angelic lump in the cage seemed to weave into Herself slowly, a gray bundle of old ropes slipping from a great knot. Smaller and smaller and smaller.

And then, Despair was gone.

Death slumped, breathing hard for several seconds. She seemed to gather Herself, stood straight. She turned to me with a tired look that slowly tightened to a hunter's stare, then softened into bedroom eyes.

A few calm steps and She was standing inches from me. I could feel the chill from Her breasts through my shirt.

"You're out of bullets, Charlie."

"Despair is no longer here, Gorgeous."

I tossed the spent pistol aside.

"And, I'm no longer afraid of You."

She laid Her arms over my shoulders and tilted Her head to one side.

"So now what? Are you fearless enough to give Me the kiss I wanted before?"

She eased forward until there was no more forward to be eased into.

"You were lying about knowing everything, weren't You?"

"Mmm," She shrugged, grinning in Her mischief. "There is a brief moment, right before the flame finally goes out."

She blinked slowly, like a sleepy cat.

"But in the end, Charles, knowledge is of the material world. It dies with the body."

"You take it all?"

"I catch everything, sweetie."

I thought about all of it, about my detective agency, my neighborhood, my city, my life. No more long-lost relatives, no more ancestry nuts. No more suspicious conspiracy theorists and their sweeps for government bugs.

No more chasing after Núr's silly quests, or Curiosity's endless wrong turns. No more wrangling with angels, and getting ambushed on the brambly borders between religions.

No more hiding. No more denial. No more Safe New World, where a Rough like me just doesn't fit in.

I felt the chill of Her lips parting, Her tongue against mine.

Case closed.

ON THE HEAD OF A PIN